Foxglove

Jean Ure

This book is dedicated to the Wandle Valley
Wildlife Hospital, Beddington Park, Croydon.
With thanks

Scholastic Children's Books,
Commonwealth House,
1-19 New Oxford Street,
London WC1A 1NU, UK
A division of Scholastic Ltd
London ~ New York ~ Toronto ~ Sydney ~ Auckland

First published in the UK by Scholastic Ltd, 1998

Copyright © Jean Ure, 1998

ISBN 0 590 19531 X

Typeset by
Cambrian Typesetters, Frimley, Camberley, Surrey
Printed by
Cox and Wyman Ltd, Reading, Berkshire

10 9 8 7 6 5 4 3 2 1

Chapter 1

O ne night when I was asleep, having this mega ace dream about living in the middle of a field surrounded by animals (which actually is my ambition in life), I was rudely awoken by Mum hissing "Clara!" right into my ear.

I immediately shot up the bed going "What, what?" thinking at the very least the house must be on fire. Mud shot with me. Mud is my dog – well, mine and Jilly's – and we always sleep together. It's brilliant in winter as we snuggle up close and it stops you sh-sh-sh...ivering, though sometimes in summer I have to push him away as dog fur is really *hot*.

This, however, was January, and so we were both huddled as deep as could be beneath the duvet.

"Here!" Mum held out my dressing-gown. "Put this on and come very very quietly over to the window. There's something you'd like to see."

I was really mystified! What could she want me to look at on a cold winter's night? It was freezing outside, and quite freezing indoors, as well. We don't have any central heating in our ancient old cottage. I wasn't surprised when Mud dived back under the duvet. He's not stupid!

"Look." Mum pointed down into the garden. "By the dustbin. See?"

At first I couldn't make anything out, but then a small dark shape slid into view and went trotting off up the garden.

"Oh!"

I stared, entranced. It was a fox! A beautiful fox! The very first one that I had ever seen. And it was in *our garden*!

Mum and I stood silently at the window, watching as it nosed about by the shed.

"It must be looking for food," said Mum. "It was trying to get into the bin. That's what woke me."

"Could we take it some?"

Mum shook her head. "You'd only frighten it off."

"It's so gorgeous!"

And so *tiny*. I was amazed how tiny it was! I hadn't realized that foxes were so small. Smaller by far than Mud, though admittedly he is quite a large sort of dog, with rather long, gangly legs. The fox's legs were quite thin and spindly. She (I felt it had to be a vixen, because surely a dog fox would be bigger?) had a very sharp, pointy muzzle and a thick bushy tail (which I now know is called a brush), that she carried quite differently from the way Mud carries his. Mud's tail is either *up* or *down*. The little fox's tail was quite near to the ground, and when she moved she seemed almost to crouch and hug the earth.

"There!" said Mum. "Our very first visitor!"

The first that we knew of, anyway. When you have a big bouncing dog like Mud it tends to scare away any daytime wildlife; and at night, when the place could be absolutely teeming, you're boringly tucked up in bed and never see anything.

"Mum, can I ring Jilly?" I begged.

Jilly lives next door and is my best friend. My *very* best friend. We are seriously into animals and I knew that she would be just as excited by the sight of that little vixen as I was, but Mum said I couldn't possibly go ringing people up at two o'clock in the morning just to look at foxes.

"Jilly wouldn't mind!" I said. In fact she'd probably never forgive me if I *didn't* ring her.

I pointed this out to Mum but Mum said, "Clara, you can't! It's enough to give people heart attacks when the phone rings in the middle of the night. One always imagines that something terrible has happened."

"I wouldn't!" I said. "I'd think I'd won the lottery."

"In that case, you'd be disappointed. Just be thankful I woke you! You can tell Jilly all about it in the morning."

With that I had to be content. But I couldn't help thinking how cross Jilly was going to be! We always share everything, the two of us. Even Mud.

Mum and I watched as the fox delicately

picked up one paw and stood, sniffing the air. She obviously decided there was nothing worth having, for after a few seconds she turned and loped off towards the back wall. The funny thing is that *Mud* can't jump that wall, or at any rate he's never tried to. But that little fox was up and over with hardly any effort at all.

"She'll be heading for the golf course," said Mum.

"Do foxes live on golf courses?" I said.

"In the woods. You know there's all that woodland there? That's probably where she's come from."

I think Mum was just as delighted at seeing the fox as I was! It took me ages to get back to sleep. I kept remembering the way she'd stood there, with her lovely pointy snout raised, sniffing the air. And the way she'd slunk back across the garden, keeping so low that her tail almost trailed the ground.

Next morning when we let Mud out he went almost berserk, running all about with his nose quivering. Mum discovered that the clever fox had actually overturned the dustbin and dragged out the contents in search of food. Unfortunately there wasn't very much in there that would be of any interest to a fox, except an old picked chicken carcass from Mum and Benjy's Sunday dinner. (Being animal people, Jilly and me are veggies, but we haven't yet managed to convince our mums. We are working on them!)

Anxiously I said, "Was there anything left on it?"

"Not a lot," said Mum.

"Oh." I had visions of the poor fox starving, what with the weather being so cold and the ground being so frozen.

"It probably crunched up the bones," said Mum. "It doesn't seem to have left much."

"But I thought chicken bones weren't supposed to be good for them!" Mud isn't ever allowed them. The vet says they could splinter in his insides and make him ill.

"Maybe foxes can cope," said Mum.

I told Jilly about our night-time adventure when we took Mud for his walk later that morning. It was Saturday, so we went for a good long one across the fields. Poor Jilly! She was ever so envious. I knew she would be.

"I wanted to ring you," I said, "but Mum wouldn't let me. She said it would give your mum a heart attack."

"Oh, it's so unfair!" wailed Jilly. "Will it come back again, do you think?"

I said I thought it might, because of the chicken carcass. If it had found something once, it might hope to find something again.

Jilly said, "We could leave food out for it!"

"Yes," I said, "and then if it comes..." I stopped. I'd been going to say, "this time I'll let you know." But how would I be able to? If Mum wouldn't let me ring? And how would I know that the fox was there anyway, unless I sat up waiting?

"We could stay awake and keep watch," said Jilly. "I'll do it. I don't mind." She was really determined to see that fox!

"We'll take it in turns," I said. "Me one night and you the next. But I don't see how we're going to wake each other."

We put our heads together and finally hatched

up our fox-watching plan. We would leave it some food (down by the dustbin, because that was where it had found some before, and because Jilly could see our bin from her window) and we would take it in turns to set our alarm clocks for quarter-to two. Then if the fox came, whoever was on watch would let the other know by banging on the wall.

"I could have done that last night," I said.

"Yes, but then I wouldn't have known what you were doing it for. Let's go and see if it works!"

Our cottage is one of four and Jilly's is right next door. They are joined together, and Jilly and me both sleep in the same room at the back. (Our mums are at the front, while Benjy, who is my little brother, sleeps in a tiny weeny room like a cupboard.)

"You bang on the wall," said Jilly, "then I'll bang back to show that I've heard you."

I *thumped* on that wall but Jilly never banged back. So I ran across and flung open the window and there was Jilly's head sticking out and she yelled, "Why haven't you banged?" and I said, "I have banged! I nearly knocked the wall down!" and she said, "Well, *I* didn't hear you."

So then I went back and did it again, and this time I did it with the heel of a shoe and Jilly heard it and so did Mum. Mum yelled up the stairs, "Clara, for goodness' sake! You'll bring the ceiling down!" So *that* wasn't going to work.

Jilly then had a bright idea, which was something she'd read in a book when she was younger.

"There were these kids and they wanted to wake each other up for a midnight feast so they tied bits of string to their toes and one of them tugged on it."

Sim-pul! No noise, no problem. Just get a bit of string—

And do what, exactly? How do you get a bit of string out of one window and into another?

"How did they do it in the book?"

"I don't remember," confessed Jilly. "I think perhaps they were all in the same place. Like it was a boarding school, or something."

"Oh! Well. *That's* a lot of help."

"Maybe we could—"

"What?"

"Well, maybe we could—"

"Climb out of my window and into yours?"

"We could tie a weight on the end of it!"

So we tied a shoe on to one end of the string and I slung it out of my window and whooshed it up at Jilly's while she leaned out and tried to catch it. The first time it nearly smashed the window, which Jilly said was my fault for whooshing too vigorously, so then I whooshed a bit more gently and Jilly had to lean out so far she nearly toppled headfirst into the garden.

So then *I* had a bright idea (I think I am quite practical, really) and suggested that we get two lengths of string and tie a shoe on to each of them and drop them both out of the windows.

"Then all we have to do is go down and take the shoes off and tie the bits of string together."

"*Yesssss!*" said Jilly.

There is always a solution if you just put your mind to it.

We cut two really *long* lengths of string, weighted them with shoes, dropped one out of my window and one out of Jilly's, then galloped downstairs to tie them together. Eeeeezeeeee!

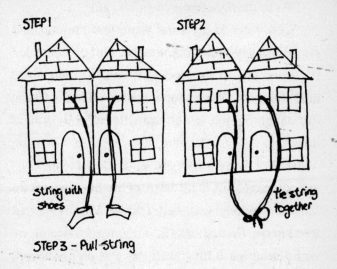

STEP 1

STEP 2

string with shoes

tie string together

STEP 3 - Pull string

"Let's try some tugging," said Jilly. "I'll go and lie on my bed and tie the string round my toe and pretend to be asleep, and you try tugging at me."

So I tugged really hard, and then ran across to the window, and Jilly stuck her head out and shrieked, "I almost fell off the bed!"

"Good," I said. "So it works!"

When we trailed back indoors for what must have been about the fifth or sixth time, Mum said, "What on earth are you two girls up to? In out, in out ... all I hear are doors banging."

"We're doing a fox project," I said.

"Well, stop doing it for just a few minutes and come and say hallo to someone. Girls!" Mum led us into the front room. "This is our new neighbour, Mr Woodvine's nephew. This is Clara, my daughter, and her friend Jilly, who lives next door."

Mr Woodvine's nephew said, "Jeff Hennessy," and shook hands with both of us in a grown-up kind of way which I liked. Old Mr Woodvine had lived in the first cottage in our row of four, but he was getting on a bit – well, he was eighty-seven, as a matter of fact – so just before Christmas he'd moved to sheltered accommodation. Jilly and me had been wondering who was going to move in and praying it wouldn't be someone who shot things or hunted things or nailed dead squirrels to trees, which alas are all things that can happen when you live in the country.

Mr Hennessy didn't *look* like a man that would nail squirrels to a tree. His face was all craggy and smiley, which made me think perhaps he had a sense of humour, and his hair sprang up in sandy-coloured tufts as if he'd slept on it the wrong way and hadn't bothered brushing it. When he shook hands it was like shaking hands with a big warm boxing glove – all squashy and firm.

Of course, you can't always go by looks. Probably lots of people that murder animals have smiley faces and tufty hair and hands like boxing gloves. You just can't tell. But the first thing Mr Hennessy said (after saying hallo) was, "I've just been admiring your hound! He's a very handsome fellow, isn't he?"

Well! Anyone who admires Mud is our friend *straight* away.

"He's deaf," said Jilly. "We rescued him."

"It's what we do," I said. "We rescue animals. We've devoted our lives to it."

"Yes, I know. Your mum was telling me. She said you're both animal mad."

"We are Animal Lovers," said Jilly.

She meant that we belong to this organization that is called Animal Lovers, but Mr Hennessy obviously hadn't heard of them because he said, "I'm a bit of an animal lover myself."

Three cheers! No one who truly loves animals can hunt or shoot them.

Or can they?

There are people who *say* that they love animals but still do terrible things to them. Like, for instance, shutting them up in hateful laboratories and torturing them. That, I think, is just so wicked it is almost unbelievable.

Even people who hunt foxes *say* that they love animals. I really did hope that Mr Hennessy wouldn't turn out to be one of those. It would be very hard, living cheek by jowl with a murderer.

"I've promised myself, now that I'm in the country, that I shall get a dog," he said.

We pounced, immediately.

"A rescued one?"

We said it together, but I got in just ahead!

Mr Hennessy said yes, it probably would be a rescued one. "Because that's the right thing to do, isn't it?"

This time, Jilly beat me to it.

"There's this sanctuary called End of the Line where we sometimes help out. They are *desperate* to find homes for all their poor dogs."

"We could take you," I said. "It's only just down the road."

"Five minutes in a car," said Jilly.

"Girls, girls!" Mum threw up her hands. "Give the poor man a chance! He's only just got here. At least let him settle in."

Mr Hennessy assured us that it wouldn't take him long.

"I travel light. Just my computer and the clothes I stand up in."

I couldn't help wondering what sort of work he did. I knew Mum would tick me off if I dared to ask but he told us anyway. What a relief! He was a writer. It would have been truly dreadful if he'd said, for instance, that he was a butcher or a gamekeeper. How could we ever have talked to him?

He said, "I scrape a living writing articles. I used to be a teacher, but it's all right, you can relax." He looked at us and laughed. "I gave that up. I only do supply teaching these days, and not even that if I can help it."

Now that he'd told us it didn't seem too rude to ask him what he wrote articles about. He said, "Anything and everything! I'm hoping to do some on the country ... wild life, that sort of thing."

"You could do one about foxes," I said. "We've got a fox that comes to our garden."

Mr Hennessy said, "Really? How splendid! Do you think it will come to mine?"

"It might," I said, "if you put some food out. That's what we're going to do."

"I would feel extremely privileged," said Mr Hennessy.

Yes! That was exactly how I felt! *Privileged*. That a wild creature should have chosen to come and visit us.

When Mr Hennessy had gone I said, "He seems like a really nice man."

Mum laughed. "You'd say that about anyone who liked Mud!"

"Didn't you think he was nice?" I said.

"Yes, I did, but you mustn't pester him. And look, if you intend leaving food out for that fox, may I just ask where you think you're going to get it from?"

"Um – well."

I flicked a glance at Jilly.

"What sort of thing do you think foxes eat?" said Jilly.

"Dog food?" I said, brightly.

"You're not using Mud's food," said Mum. "He costs quite enough to feed without you giving half of it away to the fox population. If you want to support a stray fox, you can buy it some tins out of your pocket money."

I suppose it was only fair. I tried telling Mum that what we were doing was educational – "We're going to keep diaries and record every time we see her" – but all Mum said was, "Bully for you! If you shoot off down the road now, you might still find a shop open."

When we came back, humping six cans of dog food, we found that Beastly Bernard was there. Jilly's mum always referred to him as Mum's gentleman friend; I referred to him as the Beast. I didn't like him one little bit. He was dead snooty, for one thing, and for another he trod on snails. I mean, quite *deliberately*, to crush them. I just couldn't understand what Mum saw in him.

"Ho!" he said, as me and Jilly came in. "Here's Clara with din-dins!" He was staying to eat with us, worse luck. "What do we have? Chicken and

17

liver, yum yum! I thought I might be fed on lettuce leaves now you've turned veggie."

"Mum hasn't," I said. "*Yet.*" I just bet she would have if it hadn't been for old Beastly. "And these happen to be for our fox."

"Fox?" said Beastly. "What fox?"

"There was a little fox that came into the garden last night," said Mum. "The girls want to put some food out for it."

"Shouldn't do that," said Bernard. "Foxes are vermin. You shouldn't encourage them."

I opened my mouth, indignantly, but as usual Mum stepped in. She really hated it when I argued with Bernard. (Him and me don't see eye to eye on anything, and especially not on anything to do with animals.)

"It's for a project they're doing at school."

I blinked. I hadn't said it was for school!

"Recording fox movements," said Mum.

"Well, if it's one of those from up by the golf course, they're nothing but a damned nuisance." Bernard was a golfer. Wouldn't you know it? "And what about those kittens you brought back from the dead? It'll have those, for sure!"

"No, it won't," I said, quickly, before Jilly could fly into a total panic. She and her mum had bottle-fed those kittens. Well, we'd all helped, but it had been Jilly and her mum mainly. "The kittens don't go out at night."

"You'd better make sure they don't. Foxes are killers. Kill for the fun of it. In any case, they're wild animals. They shouldn't be fed by humans."

"Birds are wild animals, too!" I retorted. "And we're always being told to feed *them*."

"Yes, and I even have my doubts about that," said Bernard. "Look at the mess those pigeons have made in the town centre. It's disgusting!"

Oh, he really was such a *horrible* man. What's a little bit of pigeon goo? Pigeons have as much right to exist as anyone else.

"Don't worry about Chalky and Smudge," I said to Jilly, as we put the dog food away. Chalky and Smudge are the kittens. Both pure white, except for a teeny little blodge of grey on Smudgie's head. "He's only saying that to frighten us. Foxes don't kill cats, I know they don't."

I'd once seen this film on television about a

19

fox on its night-time prowl coming face to face with a cat that was eating a bit of fish it had got from somewhere. The cat had puffed itself up to about three times its size and spat, horribly, and the poor old fox had turned and slunk away looking really dejected.

I told this to Jilly and she said, "Yes, I'm sure you're right." It was quite brave of her, really, because she is a bit of a worry guts.

Anyway, that night before going to bed we opened a can of dog food and put half of it near the dustbin on a tin plate. Just before two o'clock my alarm went off and I sprang across to the window. Just in time to see the little fox come slithering over the back wall and into the garden! I immediately tugged like mad at our piece of string. I knew from the answering tug that Jilly had got the message. It was good to know that both of us were watching. It wouldn't have been nearly as much fun if it had been just me by myself.

The fox made a beeline for the dustbin. She had obviously remembered! She found the dog food almost immediately. She looked all round before she crouched to eat, checking that no one was going to creep up on her, and then she wolfed the lot even quicker than Mud. She must have been *really* hungry.

After that, she moved into the middle of the garden, sat down and had a bit of a think and a bit of a scratch, then bounded off again, over the wall. I knew she was the same one as before by a white tuft at the end of her tail. I didn't think there could be all that many foxes with white tufts. And anyway, she'd gone straight for where the chicken carcass had been.

As she went over the wall, Jilly gave a tug on the string. I tugged back and scrambled into bed to make a note in my diary:

2 a.m. Fox came to visit. Same time as last night. Ate dog food then went away.

In the morning I said to Jilly, "Did you see her all right?"

Jilly said yes, and she was even more beautiful than she had imagined.

"I didn't know they were so *dainty*." Then she said, "Tonight it's my turn to set the alarm. And I'll tug you as hard as you tugged me!"

She said that I had almost strangled her big toe.

But she did agree with me that a strangulated big toe was a small price to pay for the honour of seeing a real live fox in the garden!

Chapter 2

O ur mums wouldn't let us set our alarm clocks every day because of school, but we took it in turns at weekends. On lots of nights during the cold weather we saw Foxglove delicately picking her way across the garden and taking the food that we'd left for her. When a big freeze came at the end of February we put warm water out, as well, because we knew she might find it difficult with all the ponds and lakes iced over. It made us really happy to think that this shy, wild creature had chosen *our* garden – well, mine actually, but as I said, Jilly and me always share – and that we were helping her survive.

Old Beastly Bernard said with the usual sneer in his voice that we needn't kid ourselves she'd be grateful, but we didn't expect gratitude.

Foxglove was just being a fox, doing her own foxy thing, and Jilly and me were just being humans, doing our human thing, which was getting pleasure out of watching a beautiful animal. Sometimes Mum watched with us, and once she even woke Benjy so that he could see.

It was because of Benjy that Foxglove came to be called Foxglove. Before that, she'd just been Foxy, or Foxy Loxy. I can't remember if I mentioned it, but my brother Benjy is deaf, or hard of hearing, as Mum for some reason prefers to say. (She doesn't mind us saying that Mud is deaf. I think that is a bit doggist, myself.)

One night we were all watching out of the window, me and Mum and Benje, and Jilly next door 'cos I'd given a good hefty tug on the piece of string, when in tones of wonderment Mum said, "She is exquisite! So tiny!"

We still couldn't get over how tiny she was. We'd always had this image of foxes being about the size of a big German Shepherd, which maybe perhaps a dog fox might be, but never a vixen. But we didn't know that then. We'd only lived in the country a short while. We were still townies.

"She looks hardly more than a fox cub," marvelled Mum.

Benjy said, "Pock glubb?"

"*Fox* cub," said Mum. She's always trying to get Benjy to pronounce things properly. He can, if he takes the trouble, but he doesn't always bother.

"Pock glubb," said Benjy.

"*Fox* glubb," said Mum. "F-f-*fox* gl—" And then she realized what she was saying, and why I was giggling.

"You mean foxglove," I said.

"No, I don't! I mean – oh! I give up," said Mum.

He gets you like that, Benjy does. If you're not careful you find you're talking Benjy talk, which is OK at home where we can all understand each other, but can be quite embarrassing if you forget and do it in public. Like this one time in the supermarket I cried, "Ooh, dawbi dard!" and everyone turned and looked at me. Benjy knew what I meant, all right. So did Mum. Strawberry tarts! I guess it's like a kind of secret language known only to the three of us.

Four if you count Jilly. But she's only a beginner!

Anyway, next morning when Jilly and I met up to take Mud for his walk, old Benje came dancing out and proudly announced that "I dor Pockglubb lah dide."

Jilly said, "You saw *what* last night?"

"Pockglubb," said Benjy.

"*Fox*glove?"

"Inna gardin."

"Oh! Yes. Isn't she lovely?" said Jilly.

Benjy seemed to think that Foxglove was her name, and so that was what we started calling her. We kept Foxglove charts of when she came and what she ate. During the cold weather she was in the garden most nights, even though we weren't always awake to see her. (I did try training myself to wake at quarter to two without the help of my alarm clock, but unfortunately it didn't work very often. One night I woke up and thought "Hooray! I've done it!" only to discover that it wasn't even ten o'clock. I'd been asleep for precisely *five minutes*!)

You could tell when Foxglove had visited us

26

because the food bowl would be empty. Of course we couldn't be *absolutely* certain that it was her, but we guessed that it was since she was the only one we'd ever seen.

Mud was madly jealous! He went tearing out first thing every morning like an express train, straight to the food bowl. I always tried to get there first because Mum said you never knew what diseases a fox might be carrying, and we wouldn't want Mud to catch anything nasty.

"Like mange, for instance," said Mum.

Mange is horrible. It's caused by a mite and it makes all the animal's fur fall out and they itch most terribly and get covered in disgusting crusty bits and sores, which sometimes become infected and, in the end, if they're not treated, they die most miserably in agony. When dogs get it they are taken to the vet, but most of the poor foxes are just left to perish.

If I saw a fox with mange I would do my utmost to catch it so that it could be helped, though it is not easy to catch a wild animal. Even when they are injured most dreadfully they put up a fight. This is because they are so terrified of human beings, for which I cannot say I blame them.

Foxglove, thank goodness, did not have mange. She looked bright and alert and healthy as could be, but I agreed with Mum that it wasn't wise to let Mud lick out her food bowl. He really resented me taking it off him because Mud has this big thing about foxes. One of his all-time favourite activities is to roll in fox droppings. He likes to get it in his ruff and round his ears. Mum says it's disgusting, and I must confess it does pong, rather, but to Mud it is sheer bliss. Like some kind of doggy perfume, I suppose. "Pour le chien" or "Eau de Reynard".

Jilly giggles when I say this and points out that it's not "eau" it's "poo". But she doesn't know what that is in French and neither do I!

We'd been up to the golf course several times and had discovered there were lots of fox earths up there, hidden in the woods. You could tell they were fox and not badger by the smell. Since Foxglove had been visiting us, we had learnt to recognise the smell of fox. Mum described it as "musky". I am not quite sure what this means but there was no mistaking it when you went into the garden in the early morning. I can only say that it is an *animal* smell.

I know! A bit like certain kinds of plastic. It is rather odd, that a fox should smell like plastic, but maybe that is why Mud sometimes tries to eat plastic refuse sacks and bits of plastic wrapping.

When I remarked on this to Mum she said, "Oh, that dog would eat anything!" The Beast once said that Mud was obviously first cousin to a waste disposal unit. That is *quite* funny, I suppose.

By now, Jilly and me were getting into foxes in a big way. We would have loved to have made friends with Foxglove but we knew that you should never try to tame a wild creature, even if they let you, because then they would become too trusting, which would mean they were at risk. So we had to be content with watching through the window.

Mum left the window open one night and managed to get some really good photographs, including one where Foxglove had turned and was looking up at us. Fortunately we were frozen like statues and so she probably didn't realize that we were horrible humans. Well, *we* aren't horrible as we would never dream of harming an animal but there are all too many who would.

I took the photographs into school and everyone clamoured to look at them. Most people agreed with us that Foxglove was beautiful, and thought that we were really lucky to have her come and visit us, but there were one or two who said that foxes were vermin and we shouldn't be encouraging them. We got into quite heated arguments about it.

Needless to say, Geraldine Hooper, a girl we loathe and despise, was one of those who were anti-fox. It is all you would expect of someone like her. She has an uncle who is in the fur trade and says that when she grows up she is going to wear a mink coat because mink are vicious and evil and deserve to be made into coats. If I see her, I shall throw red paint over her! I *hate* Geraldine Hooper.

She said that foxes were vicious and evil, as well. And her best friend, Puffin Portinari (who has no neck, though I suppose that is hardly her fault), said that her dad was whipper-in of the local fox hounds and *he* thought anyone that was against fox hunting was ignorant and stupid.

I said, "That means that almost everyone in this class is ignorant and stupid."

Puffin said, "Some people are just ignorant. You're stupid. You keep on about how much you love animals but you don't bother to find out the first thing about them."

"It's because they're not real country people," said Geraldine.

Jilly had gone all red. She said to Puffin, "Just what do you mean, exactly?"

"I mean you're ignorant and stupid!" screeched Puffin. She'd gone all red, as well. "Haven't you ever heard of foxes breaking into hen-houses and tearing all the hens to pieces?"

"And lambs," said Geraldine.

I was a bit shaken, to tell the truth, and couldn't immediately think what to say. But Jilly was really quick. She said, "Foxes have to eat! They're carnivores. They're programmed that way."

"Unlike human beings," I said, suddenly

remembering that since Christmas Jilly and me had been one hundred per cent veggie. "Human beings only *choose* to be carnivores."

"Yes, and human beings kill loads more animals than foxes do!"

"Only for food," said Puffin.

"Precisely!" Geraldine looked at us, all triumphant, as if she'd scored some kind of point. "Human beings kill to eat. Foxes just kill for the sake of killing."

"They do. It's true." That was Darren Bickerstaff joining in the argument. He said it sort of apologetically. As if he didn't really want to come in on Geraldine's side but felt that he had to. "We had chickens once and a fox got in and killed the lot. Bit their heads off and just left 'em there. It was horrible. My mum cried when she saw it."

"You were probably only going to eat them, anyway," muttered Jilly, but I could see that for once even she had run out of things to say.

It worried me, all these accusations against foxes, especially as I didn't know whether they were true or not. I thought that ludicrous No-Neck was right for once, and that Jilly and I *were* ignorant.

"It's a pity about Darren," said Jilly, as we cycled home from school that afternoon.

"Yes." I nodded, sadly. Once upon a time we had thought Darren Bickerstaff was just a loutish yob like George Handley, another boy in our class. But then he'd helped us rescue Chalky and Smudge when they were just tiny kittens a few days old and we'd discovered that under his big, butch exterior he was really quite a softie. So it was a real blow that he had sided with old Geraldine and No-Neck.

"How can we find out?" I said.

"About foxes?"

"Mm."

Part of the trouble with living in the country is that you can't just walk up the road to the library whenever you feel like it. We have to wait for one of our mums to take us in by car. We do have a school library, of course, but it is full of these really old, grotty books from yonks ago, the sort of books that my gran would have probably read when she was young. It's not their fault, I know that; they haven't any money. But it does make life difficult when you suddenly want to find out about something and you can't.

I told Mum about Geraldine and No-Neck and she said, "You have to accept, Clara, that there are lots of different views about these things."

"Yes, but which one is *right*?" I said.

Mum suggested that maybe there wasn't just one that was right and all the rest wrong.

"It all depends where you're coming from."

I thought she meant, like, whether you came from the town or from the country, but Mum said, "No, I mean what your standpoint is. A sheep farmer, for instance, might see things quite differently from, say, a vegetarian like you."

"But being a vegetarian is right," I said. I had most firmly come to this conclusion. "Eating meat is cruel, and I don't see that cruelty can ever be right."

Mum laughed and shook her head and said, "Oh, you're an extremist!"

"Well, I am," I said, "if it means sticking up for animals."

I wanted so much to stick up for foxes, and our beautiful Foxglove, but I could see that if you went down to your hen-house one morning and found all the hens with their heads torn off it would be rather terrible.

On the other hand, as Jilly had said, Darren's mum was only going to do just the same thing herself in the end. When the hens had stopped laying, she'd only have killed them.

Jilly said that she'd read this article in an animal magazine about chickens having their throats cut. She said they'd all been hung up by their legs on a conveyor belt and their throats had been slashed as they went round.

"That's every bit as cruel as anything a fox could do!"

She said she wished she'd thought of saying this to Geraldine and No-Neck and that next time she *would* say it. And then she said, "Why don't we ring up Hen Haven?"

Well! That was a truly brilliant idea. Hen Haven is this chicken and turkey sanctuary where we'd taken Trevor, a Christmas turkey that had been left on our doorstep with a note saying

"Please don't eat me". They would know about foxes killing chickens, if anyone did!

So we rang them up, and Jim, the lovely man who runs the place, said it was true that if you kept chickens all cooped up together and a fox got in, the chances were the fox would get madly over-excited, what with all the poor birds rushing dementedly to and fro, clucking and squawking, and might well go on a killing spree.

"The point is, chickens shouldn't be cooped up like that. It's not natural. They should be left free to range, as ours are. That way, the fox will just take what it needs. You can hardly blame it for that! That's nature."

He then added that if we could put men on the moon we certainly ought to be able to build fox-proof hen-houses if we insisted on having such things.

"Anyone who lets a fox get into a hen-run has only themselves to blame. Don't get on the fox's case!"

We were really glad that we'd talked to Jim as we now felt we had enough ammunition with which to fight our enemies. We flung it at them next day, but they refused to listen. Old No-Neck just snapped, "It doesn't alter the facts," and Geraldine shouted, "What about lambs?"

"What about them?" said Jilly.

"Foxes kill them! They bite their throats out!"

"Yes, and men do things that are even worse! *They* cram them into lorries and take them over to the Continent to be slaughtered!"

Jilly was putting up a really good fight and I felt guilty because I wasn't contributing, but my heart was sinking again because *everyone* accuses foxes of killing lambs and I just couldn't think of a single thing to say. We still didn't know enough to argue properly. Geraldine, meanwhile, was all flushed and triumphant, feeling she'd come out on top again.

"Foxes are *pests*. They have to be *controlled*."

Darren said, "Yeah, I reckon they do and I reckon hunting's the best way to do it. Better 'n gassing."

"*Gassing?*" shrieked Jilly.

"Well, or snaring. That's real cruel, that is."

Jilly and I agreed that the whole thing was utterly depressing.

"I can't understand why people want to kill all the time!" wailed Jilly.

It was shortly after this heated debate that Foxglove stopped visiting us. You can imagine how worried we were. We had these terrible visions of her being gassed or caught in a snare.

We confided our fears to Meg, at End of the Line, when we went to help out one Sunday. Meg is such a comfort! I think she is what is known as a Fount of Wisdom.

She said, "It's true that this is hunting country but I haven't heard of snares being used in a long time, or gassing. I shouldn't fret too much. If it's a vixen, she's probably just given birth. Foxes have their litters round about now. She'll be lying up in her den with the dog fox bringing the food in. There's rabbits and voles and all sorts of things he can get at this time of year, so don't expect any more visits for just a while."

"Will she come back again, do you think?"

"She might well. Give her a month or two, she might even bring her cubs to see you."

So we stopped putting food out and waking ourselves up in the early hours of the morning every Friday and Saturday and growing agitated because Foxglove no longer visited. I wrote in my diary:

It is the breeding season when Vixens have their litters and stay in their dens and the dog fox brings the food.

I had this idyllic picture of Foxglove curled up in a nest of leaves safe underground, with all her cubs about her, while a big handsome dog fox attended to her every need. Or sometimes I pictured her lying outside the den, basking in the sunshine, with the cubs jumping and playing and the dog fox proudly watching.

I even took one of Mum's photographs, where Foxglove was sitting in the middle of the garden, and cut her out and stuck her on a sheet of paper together with some pictures of fox cubs that I'd found. I then coloured in some grass and flowers and a lovely blue sky and pinned it to my bedroom wall where I could see it first thing when I woke in the morning.

Jilly said, "I wish I'd thought of that!"

I said that when Foxglove came back we would take some more photographs and Jilly could make a picture of her own.

"Do you really think she will come back?" said Jilly.

I didn't know but I firmly said yes, because I do believe in looking on the bright side. I mean, it can't hurt and it's better than making yourself miserable by always imagining the worst.

"I hope she does," said Jilly. "I'd hate not knowing what's happened to her."

You just can never tell when disaster is going to strike.

With Jilly and me, it was Easter Sunday. We were out with Mud, walking through a grassy field full of wild flowers. Little pinky things, and yellow things, and some that were brightest blue. So pretty! So peaceful! Mud was snuffling to and fro, doing his own thing. Jilly and me, we were just being happy.

Then all of a sudden we heard the sound of horses, and the braying of a horn, and before we knew it the field was full of red-faced men in pink coats, and hatchet-faced women in bowler hats, with their hair done up in hair nets, all on great huge galloping horses, with dozens of hounds, tails waving and noses to the ground.

I screamed, and went plunging after Mud before he could get mown down or attacked by the dogs. I only just snatched him in time as the first of the hunters thundered down on us. Jilly screeched, "Murderers!" and shook her fist. It might almost have been funny if it hadn't been so utterly horrible.

I was a bit trembly, because of poor Mud almost being trampled, but I thought I ought to support her so I yelled murderer, too.

A fat perspiring creep on a horse as tall as a house raised his crop and snarled, "Get out the way!" and a boy following behind made a rude gesture. I mean, a *really* rude gesture. Jilly screamed, "I hope you fall off your horse and break your neck!" which I daresay some people might not approve of, but which I personally thought was *exactly* what ought to happen.

And then the horn brayed again and the hounds started this hideous baying, enough to make your

41

blood curdle. The hunt swung round and began milling to and fro, while the hounds worked the ground, tails waving excitedly like flags.

As we stood watching, too terrified to move, with me clutching for dear life at Mud's collar, a small dark shape shot out from the hedge at the far end of the field and went streaking for the nearest exit. It raced past us, its muzzle wide open in a grimace of fear, the hounds in loud pursuit.

And oh! It had a white tip to its tail! It was our little Foxglove.

Chapter 3

I sobbed and sobbed when we got back home. "She was so frightened, Mum! She was absolutely terrified!"

Mum did her best to comfort me. She pointed out that not every hunt ends in a kill and that it was quite possible Foxglove could have escaped.

"But it's such a cruel thing to do," I sobbed. "Chasing some poor little fox with all those horrible dogs!"

I didn't really think they were horrible dogs; I knew it wasn't their fault. They had been set on to it by the huntsmen. But I kept seeing the fear on Foxglove's face as she streaked past us. I kept imagining her torn to pieces, nothing but a bloody mess of bones and fur. I just couldn't stop crying.

"What about her babies?" I sobbed. Those four little cubs that I had pictured her with, waiting in their den for a mum that was never going to come home. "They'll die if she's not there to feed them!"

"I expect the dog fox—" began Mum.

I turned on her, quite viciously. How could she be so *ignorant*?

"What good's he? He can't feed them! They haven't been weaned yet! They still need their mother's milk!" I sobbed all over again. "They're not just killing Foxglove, they're killing her babies, as well!"

"Oh, Clara. Come here!"

Mum folded me to her and stroked my hair, like she hadn't done since I was really tiny. I am not someone who blubs on the slightest provocation. I mean, I've broken my arm and never cried. I've had *stitches* and never cried. I did cry a bit when Dad left home. Well, to be honest I cried quite a lot when Dad left home, but nothing like the oceans I shed that day we saw our poor Foxglove pursued by the hunt.

I'm not saying I cared more about Foxglove

than I did about my dad. But at least I knew that Dad was still alive and well, even if he was living in another part of the country. I could always speak to him on the telephone, or get on a train and go and visit him. With Foxglove it was nothing but violence and pain and terror. It all swirled about inside me till I thought I would go mad and start screaming.

"Oh, Clara, Clara!"

Mum held me close until at last I stopped shaking.

"I am seriously beginning to wonder," she said, "whether moving to the country was a wise thing to do."

"What?" I shoved my hair back behind my ears. "Why?"

"If it's going to upset you so much."

"We can't move back to town!" I said. What would happen to Mud? He's too big a dog to live in a flat and go for sedate walks in the park. And anyway, there was Jilly. "Mum, please! We can't!"

"I don't want to," said Mum. "But equally I don't want you being unhappy all the time."

"I'm not *all* of the time." I scrubbed at my eyes. "Just when people are cruel!"

Mum let me stay up really late that night and watch two of my favourite videos. One was *101 Dalmations*, which Dad had given me for Christmas, and the other was *The Jungle Book*, which I thought I'd grown out of but discovered that I hadn't. Mum said it would be a good one to end the evening with.

"I don't want you watching anything miserable!"

I didn't go to bed till midnight, by which time I was pretty tired. Mum made me drink a glass of warm milk, which I loathe, but she promised that it would help me sleep and it did. Instead of lying awake worrying about Foxglove and imagining all the terrible things that could have happened to her, which was what I had been dreading, I fell asleep almost at once and stayed asleep right round till morning.

I felt almost guilty next day when Jilly came round and said that she had been awake all night, and that she'd had these horrible nightmares about Mud being trampled to death by a thousand horses. I didn't quite see how she could have been awake *and* having nightmares, but I didn't say anything because her eyes were all red and I didn't want to start us both weeping again.

It was Easter Monday and we were on school holiday. Our mums had decided to be on holiday, too. They were going off to some boring flower show with Beastly Bernard, leaving Jilly and me to look after Benje. Mum said, "You could always come with us if you want," but I think she was secretly glad when we told her that we weren't interested in flowers. It meant she wouldn't have to be worried all the time that I might be rude to the Beast or that he would say something to provoke me.

It seemed that me and the Beast just couldn't help rubbing each other up the wrong way. I guess it was because of our having these totally different attitudes towards life. Like I think animals are just as important as human beings while he thinks they are lowly creatures put on earth for us to do what we like with. I told him that that was arrogant and species-ist, and he said

47

I was just being sentimental. Mum, as usual, said I was being rude, but he got me so *mad*.

When he came round to pick up my mum and Jilly's in his big posh car he said, "Hallo, Clara! You're looking rather down. You don't seem to be your usual perky self. What's the problem?"

I wasn't going to tell him. I don't think Mum would have done, either. But Jilly's mum was there and probably she didn't quite realize about this war that went on all the time between him and me. She said, "The girls are a bit upset. They were nearly mown down in High Meadow yesterday by the local hunt."

"Hounds in full cry can be rather an awesome sight," agreed the Beast. "But I'm sure you wouldn't have been in any real danger."

"Mud was," I said.

"Yes, and so was Foxglove!" It came bursting out of Jilly in a great accusing cry. "They were chasing her!"

"Oh dear, oh dear," said the Beast. "That's the one you've been feeding? I knew no good would come of it. Now I suppose you've got it into your heads that all huntsmen are vicious and cruel?"

I said, "They are! You can't deny it! Nobody can say it's not cruel to chase an animal until it's exhausted and then tear it to pieces!"

"They don't do it for the fun of it," said Bernard. "They do it because foxes need to be controlled."

"Who says so?" I said. Rudely. I *knew* it was rude, but I just didn't care.

"Farmers?" said Bernard. "Honestly, you townies!" He shook his head. "You move into the country expecting it to be all sweetness and light. Dear little cuddly fox cubs, cheeky little squirrels, fluffy bunny rabbits, all living together in perfect bliss like some kind of Walt Disney movie."

I opened my mouth say "No, I don't," but he just ploughed straight on.

"I'm afraid nature isn't like that. Your dear little fox would have had no hesitation in tearing a rabbit to pieces or biting the head off a chicken. So if she's chased and caught by hounds, it's all in the nature of things."

I opened my mouth yet again, but this time it was Mum who jumped in. Hastily she said, "I'm sure Clara accepts that country ways are different from town ways, but until one gets used to it it can be rather disturbing."

"Of course," purred the Beast, all smooth and silky. "That's understandable. But you mustn't think you can come here and start lecturing everybody, young lady! You'll make yourself very unpopular."

As if I cared!

"I don't want to be popular," I grumbled to Jilly, after our mums had left and we were on our own. "I just want to stop people being cruel to animals!"

Jilly, who can be quite wise sometimes, said she thought that maybe anyone who wanted to change things was always going to be a bit unpopular.

"Like the suffragettes," she said. "When they were fighting to get the vote for women. Lots of people hated them. They were shut in prison and had tubes put down them."

"Tubes?" I said, startled. "What was that for?"

"To force them to eat," said Jilly. "They put them all the way down into their stomachs and pumped food in."

The thought of being in prison didn't bother me so much (apart from being separated from darling Mud) but I must admit the idea of a tube coiling right the way down into my stomach made me feel a bit queasy. All the same, I thought that I would be prepared to face it if it meant I was helping animals.

Jilly said that she would, too.

"Because we've sworn! Let's go into my place and take Mud with us so he can play with the kittens."

The kittens adore Mud! They hurled themselves at him with little catty squeaks of delight. We watched them for a bit, then Jilly said she thought they ought to go into the garden. She said, "Poor Mud's tired." It was true he'd been for a long walk, and the kittens were such skittery little things. They never knew when enough was enough. So Jilly put them outside and she and I went up to her room to look through some animal magazines that someone had given us and Benjy stayed downstairs watching television, with Mud.

Jilly and I were going to make a thing called a collage (which is pronounced "collahj", ever so lahdi dah, on account of its being French). We were going to make a wild animal scene. We were busy cutting out pictures of hedgehogs when Benjy suddenly came bursting into the room and gabbled, "Deyda liddoo mowd wunnin wowd in thurdoo."

"There's a little *what*?" I said.

"Liddoo mowd."

"Little mouse? Where?"

"Inna gardin."

"Doing what?"

"*Wunnin*," said Benjy. "In *thurdoo*."

And he went chugging off in a circle to show us what he meant.

"It's probably just having fun," said Jilly, but we supposed we'd better go and look.

When we got there I almost wished we hadn't. Just outside the back door, a tiny little brown mouse was racing frantically round and round, spinning on the spot on one back leg.

"What's the matter with it?" shrieked Jilly.

Benjy said he thought one of the kittens had got it.

"Where are the kittens?" I said.

They were back indoors, wouldn't you know it, curled up with Mud and looking positively angelic. Meanwhile, that poor little mouse was still tearing round in circles, like a clockwork toy. Every now and then it would stagger and almost come to a stop, but then something in its brain seemed to go "click!" and then off it went.

"It'll die of exhaustion!" said Jilly.

We didn't know what to do. We rang Meg at End of the Line and she said that from the sound of things it had obviously been brain-damaged beyond any hope of recovery.

"You mean there's nothing we can do?" I said, dismayed. I'd been hoping she'd say just keep the kittens away and the mouse would finally wear itself out and go to sleep and when it woke up it would be better.

"I'm sorry," said Meg. "But sometimes you just have to admit defeat. This sounds like one of those times. The kindest thing would be to put it out of its misery."

She meant kill it.

"How?" I whispered.

"Well, I know it sounds terribly brutal, but if

you could find something like a house brick, or a shovel, and simply ... bash it over the head..."

There was a pause.

"You would have to do it really hard," said Meg. "You would have to make sure that you killed it quickly and cleanly."

"D-do you—" I swallowed. Jilly was listening, with an agonized expression on her face. "Do you really think that's the kindest thing to do?"

"Yes, I do," said Meg. "I really do."

"You don't think if we just left it, it would get better?"

"Not from the way you've described it."

I heaved a big trembly sigh. "All right," I said.

We found a spade in the garden shed. We dragged it out. We went back to the mouse and we sent Benjy indoors. And then we looked at each other, waiting for one of us to be brave enough to do what had to be done.

And neither of us could. We wrung our hands and we wailed and beat our fists against our heads, but we just couldn't bring ourselves to put that little creature out of its misery.

In the end, we were such cowards, we shut

ourselves indoors and prayed that it would die without us having to take any action. But when we opened the door again, just a crack, and peered out half an hour later, there it was, still running in its circle.

"Oh, God!" moaned Jilly. "Please let it stop!"

"We've got to do something." I said. And then I thought, "Mud!" Mud has greyhound in him. He has wolfhound, too. Surely he would kill a mouse? Quickly and cleanly, like Meg had said?

I tore back indoors, seized Mud by his ruff and dragged him into the kitchen and across to the back door.

"Mud! Look! There!" I held his head between my hands so that he was pointing in the right direction. And then I let him go.

I really thought that he would leap on that poor demented mouse and snap! That would be that. The end of all its suffering. I thought that Mud would do what Jilly and I couldn't bring ourselves to.

Instead, he crept up to it ever so slowly, ever so cautiously, lowered his head to sniff at it, put out a paw to dab at it – and sprang back in alarm as it went spinning off in yet another circle.

"Please, Mud, please!" I prayed. I never, ever thought that I would pray for Mud to be a killer. And he wasn't. He watched for a bit, from a respectful distance, then looked up at me as if to say, "What do you want me to do?"

There just wasn't any way that Mud was going to kill.

"He's too much of a gentleman," said Jilly, sadly.

"It's those wicked kittens!" I said.

Jilly sighed. "Nature red in tooth and claw."

"You what?" I said.

"Nature red in tooth and claw. It means – well!" Jilly looked at the poor spinning mouse and her lips quivered. "It means that nature isn't always very nice."

"I know *that*!" I said.

What I didn't know was what to do about it. But I knew that one of us had to do something.

I took a deep breath. I picked up the spade. I raised it above my head—

And at that moment Mum's voice called

"Clara! Are you there?" and Mum's head appeared over the fence. I yelled, "Mum, there's a mouse that's been hurt and I can't kill it!"

Next thing I knew, my mum and Jilly's mum and Beastly Bernard had all appeared at the kitchen door. Bernard said, "Give it to me," and he took the spade off me and whacked it down, WHAM! right on top of the mouse. Jilly gave a little shriek, I turned the other way and Bernard, with an air of satisfaction, as if he actually enjoyed killing mice by whacking them over the head with a spade, said, "There you are! You just have to be bold."

Later on, when Bernard had gone and we were alone, Mum said, "It's just as well that he was there because I don't think I could have done it."

I knew that what she was trying to say was that I ought to be grateful to him. But although I was relieved that he'd put an end to the mouse's misery, it still didn't make me like him. I felt he could just as easily have bashed it over the head even if it hadn't been suffering.

I said this to Mum and she said, "Well, maybe

you're right, but there are times when one needs a man like that."

Mum might think that she needs one. Not me! I made a vow, right there and then, that if ever again an animal needed to be helped out of its suffering, I would be brave and not hesitate.

It is all part and parcel of being an Animal Lover.

Chapter 4

Next morning, as usual, we took Mud for his walk. We didn't go through High Meadow any more; it was too upsetting. Instead, we went through the fields and over to Crumbledown Lakes, which is a place we usually avoid on account of people fishing there.

Jilly and me think that fishing is every bit as cruel as fox hunting or bull fighting, but the boys in our class become extremely angry when you try and explain to them. They jeer at us and call us spoilsports and other names that aren't quite so nice. George Handley told us once that we had better keep our big mouths shut or he would bash us (he's a very violent sort of boy), and Puffin Portinari said we were fish freaks. To which Geraldine, thinking herself very smart, said, "*Fish* freaks? Just *freaks*."

Even big softie Darren liked to stick maggots on the end of a rod and drop it in the water, waiting for some unsuspecting fish to come by thinking, "Goody goody, here's some grub," only to get a hateful sharp hook stuck in its mouth. He just didn't seem to see anything wrong with it. Jilly and me found it dreadfully depressing.

I guess we were in a bit of a depressed sort of mood right then, what with worrying about Foxglove and being upset over the mouse. I told Jilly what Mum had said, about how maybe it hadn't been wise to come and live in the country. I thought Jilly would immediately go, "She's not thinking of moving back again?" and then I would reassure her and remind her that I had *pledged* to stay and fight for animals. But she was really down. She just said glumly that maybe Mum was right.

"What do you mean?" I said, horrified. I couldn't bear the thought that Jilly was going to desert me!

"Maybe we're too sentimental," said Jilly.

Very fiercely I said, "I don't call it sentimental to care about cruelty!"

"No, but if we can't even kill a *mouse*..."

We'd come out of the fields and were walking past the lakes. Two small boys were sitting there dangling rods in the water.

"Cruelty wherever you go!" cried Jilly. "Don't you know that fishing's cruel?" she shouted.

The boys looked at her as if she were loopy. They were only tiny little things, not much older than Benjy.

"Fish have feelings too, you know!" yelled Jilly.

One of the kids, ever so earnestly, said, "We don't kill 'em. We put 'em back again."

"So why catch them in the first place?" shrieked Jilly. "I suppose you think it's fun to torture living creatures?"

I could see that those little kids were really bemused. This mad girl was bawling at them and they hadn't the faintest idea what they were doing wrong. I plucked at Jilly's sleeve.

"Leave them," I said, "They probably won't catch anything." I mean, as a rule I'm every bit as up-front as she is, sometimes even more so, but

61

they were only tiny little kids. She was really upsetting them.

"Yes, but they're really upsetting the fish," grumbled Jilly, as I dragged her away. "What's the matter with you?"

"I think we should have talked to them nicely," I said.

"I'm not feeling nice!" Tears welled in Jilly's eyes. "I keep having these nightmares about Foxglove! I wake up in the middle of the night and I think about her and then I can't get to sleep again and I want to go and *kill* people. People that do that sort of thing. I hate them!"

"Me, too," I said.

"Why do they want to? What do they get out of it? What—"

"Eh!"

One of the little kids was rushing after us.

"That your dog?" he said. "I fink 'e's drowning!"

Mud! We had forgotten all about him! We turned and went charging frantically back.

"What happened?" gasped Jilly.

"I dunno. 'E just jumped in."

Mud was in the middle of the lake, helplessly thrashing with his front legs and rolling over and over. I didn't wait. I didn't even stop to see how deep it was, I just went diving in. Jilly dived with me. The water came up to our knees – to our waists – to our armpits – to our *shoulders*. And then at last we had reached him and were hauling him back out, on to dry land.

The two little kids sat watching, their eyes round as saucers and their mouths agape.

"Is 'e drowned?" said one.

As if in reply, Mud lowered his head, sneezed, then shook himself vigorously – brrrrrrrrrrrrrrrrrr! – sending a shower of droplets all over us.

"Oh, *Mud*!" I threw my arms round him and snuffled into his wet ruff. "Oh, Mud! You frightened me!"

"Why can't 'e swim?" said the kid who'd run after us. "I got a dog. 'E can swim. Why can't yours?"

I didn't know the answer to that. I'd always thought that all dogs could swim.

"Maybe it's because he's deaf," I said.

It was the only thing I could think of.

"If I 'adn't've called yer," said the kid, "'e might 'ave bin dead."

He would have been. The water was far too deep for those little boys to have gone to his rescue. It would have come way over their heads.

"You saved his life," I told them, and they looked ever so pleased. "We're really grateful," I said.

Jilly mumbled yes, we were; we were *really* grateful. She didn't actually say "And I'm sorry I yelled at you," but I knew she was feeling bad about it. Jilly really isn't a yelling sort of person. It was only because she was still so upset over Foxglove.

As we prepared to go on our wet watery way (with Mud on the lead, just in case) Jilly said, "I'm not nagging at you, but fish *do* have feelings. Honestly!"

"Yes, imagine how you would feel," I said, "if you had a hook stuck into the roof of your mouth."

I think that is the way to tackle it. Now those little kids would think about it every time they caught a fish and, maybe one day like us, decide that it was cruel and would stop doing it. Anyway, that is how I look at it.

"It is very odd," I remarked to Jilly, "that Mud can't swim. I never heard of a dog that couldn't. I mean, they usually do it automatically."

Jilly suddenly stopped.

"I just thought of something," she said.

"What?"

"I can't swim, either!" She giggled, rather nervously. "Can you?"

I can, as a matter of fact. But if I couldn't, would I have done what Jilly had done? She'd gone plunging into the water with me, never bothering to stop and think how deep it might be. I thought she'd been really brave, and I told her so. But I also knew that our mums would be horrified.

"We'd better not say anything about you jumping in," I said. "Just me. We'll say that Mud shook himself and that's why you're soaking."

"We could say that I *helped*," begged Jilly.

I could see that she didn't want me to hog all the honour and glory, and I could understand that, since Jilly had actually been far braver than I had.

She had been *really* brave. So I said, "I know! We'll say we formed a human chain."

"Yes." Jilly beamed. She liked that idea!

When I got home, all wet and stinky, with Mud even wetter and stinkier, Mum cried, "Oh! Is that dog doomed to live up to his name?" (We'd originally called him Mud because we'd rescued him from a ditch of muddy water.) "What have you been up to this time?"

I told her about Mud nearly drowning and Jilly and me forming our human chain. Mum frowned and said, "It sounds to me as if you weren't keeping a proper eye on him."

"I thought he'd be able to swim," I said.

"Well, deaf dogs obviously can't. Or this one can't. Why didn't you see that he'd gone into the water?"

That made me feel a bit crestfallen. I had to admit that we'd been so taken up in our concern for Foxglove that we hadn't noticed Mud wasn't with us.

Mum said, "You have to remember, Clara, that Mud isn't like other dogs. Being deaf is a great handicap."

By now I was really downcast. If Mud had drowned, it would have been all our fault! Jilly's and mine. And we would never have forgiven ourselves.

"I know this is a difficult thing to ask," said Mum, "but if you're going to go on working for animals, you really will have to learn to be a little bit braver."

Well! I thought we'd been quite brave saving Mud from drowning, but I knew that Mum was right. Terrible things are going on all the time and you have to face up to them. It is no use letting them take over your life and turn it into one of total misery. Jilly and me had been so bound up with our own worries that we had totally forgotten our poor Mud.

Anyway, I am glad to say that two good things came out of it. The first good thing was that Jilly learnt to swim! I happened to mention to Mum that she couldn't and Mum said, "Good gracious me! An animal rescuer who can't swim? We'll have to do something about that." So she had a word with Beastly Bernard and he arranged for us to use the pool attached to the golf club and Mum took us up there every day for a whole week and gave Jilly lessons. I had to stay in the shallow end to keep an eye on Benje, with his plastic water wings. He was still at the stage of hopping along with one foot on the bottom saying, "Looga me, looga me! I'm dwimmin!"

By the end of the week Jilly really *was* swimming. She could do a whole length! She was dead proud of herself.

"So there you are. Next time Mud goes jumping into a lake you can both dive in after him," said Mum.

But it wasn't ever going to happen again. No way!

The other good thing was that when we told Meg about it she was really grateful because, like us, she had never realized that a deaf dog might not be able to swim. She said that in future she would be sure to warn people.

Thinking of Mr Woodvine's nephew, we asked her if she had any special dogs that needed re-homing at this particular moment.

"Because we know this man who is going to rescue one and he is really nice and we thought you might have one that was blind or – or had only three legs, or something."

Meg laughed and said she didn't happen to have any cripples or invalids just right now. And then, growing serious, she said, "But I do have a dog that's going to need a very special kind of home."

We asked her what it was and she said, "It's a pit bull terrier and her name's Dixie."

I saw that Jilly had turned a bit pale. Even I felt a few tremors at the mention of a pit bull.

"Aren't they killers?" I said.

"They have been bred for fighting, unfortunately. But not all of them are vicious. Dixie's as sweet as a nut! Come and see her."

She was such a strange-looking dog! She was white and brown, in patches, and had this huge great snout and simply enormous head. She was sitting in a cage, all by herself. When she opened her mouth to yawn it was quite scary because there were these two rows of incredible teeth, all interlocked, like a shark's. If she got anything clamped between them you would simply *never* get it out. But when Meg called to her she came wagging over and pressed her big head against the netting and whimpered, making it as plain as could be that she just wanted someone to take her home and love her.

"She's really no different from any other dog," said Meg. "They just have this terrible reputation." Like foxes, I thought. "And of course you do have to keep them muzzled when they're on the street, because that's the law. But she's a real poppet!"

Meg said she would have taken her herself if her bungalow hadn't already been crammed to bursting point with dogs and cats that nobody wanted.

"And she would probably be better with a man. She needs firm handling because she's a big powerful dog. She'd be too strong for you girls, for instance."

"Why is she here?" Jilly wanted to know.

"Oh, it's the same old story!" Meg pulled a face. "A new baby comes along so the dog has to go."

"I am never *ever* going to have babies," I said.

I said it again to Mum when I got home. The Beast was there – he always seemed to be there, these days. It was seriously beginning to alarm me – and needless to say he found it amusing.

"What's brought this on?" said Mum.

I started to tell her about poor Dixie, but no sooner were the words "pit bull" out of my mouth than the Beast snapped, "Devil dogs! They'd all be put down if I had my way."

"Dixie's not a devil dog," I said. "She's a darling! I'm going to ask Mr Hennessy if he'd like her."

"Clara, you mustn't go pushing at people," said Mum. "Just leave Mr Hennessy alone."

I was indignant. "I haven't even *spoken* to him since that day he came round!"

"No, well, don't try bludgeoning him into adopting a dog he might not want."

I said scathingly that Meg wouldn't let him have her if he didn't really want her. "She's not stupid!"

"She is if she's trying to re-home a pit bull," said Bernard. "In fact she's worse than stupid, she's criminally irresponsible."

I couldn't very well say anything rude after he'd let us use his rotten old golf club swimming pool for a whole week, but I did find it hard having to bite my tongue. It really worried me the way he and Mum suddenly seemed to have become an item.

I wailed at Jilly that I didn't think I could stand it if Mum actually went and married him.

"I'd sooner take Mud and go and live in a tent!"

"Well, I suppose that would be one solution," said Jilly. "If you're going to keep getting on each other's nerves all the time."

"Wouldn't he get on your nerves?" I retorted.

"Yes, but my mum hasn't got a thing about him!"

"Don't gloat," I said. "Hey, look! There's Mr Hennessy. Let's go and tell him about Dixie."

"I thought you said your mum said—"

"She did, but this is important!"

We raced down the lane and caught Mr Hennessy as he was getting into his car.

"You wouldn't like a pit bull terrier that's been got rid of because of a new baby, would you? She's as sweet as a nut," I gabbled.

Mr Hennessy blinked.

"I don't know," he said. "Would I?"

"Well, I would," I said. "She's gorgeous!"

"And she desperately needs a good home," said Jilly.

"You think I would be a good home?"

I studied him for a moment, looking at his craggy face with the funny crinkle lines round the eyes. I nodded.

"Yes," I said. "I think you would."

"I'm exceedingly flattered!" said Mr Hennessy.

"So would you like her?"

I was sure he was about to say yes! But Mum had to go and choose that moment to put in an appearance.

"Clara, I hope you're not nagging Mr Hennessy about that dog?" she said.

I said, "I'm not nagging. I'm asking."

"You mean you're bludgeoning!"

"Blackmailing, more like." Mr Hennessy grinned. He looked really fun when he did that. His face went all crumpled and rumpled and made me want to laugh. "Don't worry! I can take care of myself."

"That's not the point. They ought not to be doing it," said Mum.

"They're only trying to help the animals," said Mr Hennessy. "I admire them for that. And look, I *will* go and adopt a dog. Just as soon as I can. I have one or two business trips I have to make, and then I'll put my mind to it. I promise!"

Mum was cross as hornets with me afterwards.

"I told you not to pester him!" she said. "There are times when this animal thing makes you into a real nuisance."

As Jilly said, sometimes you just have to resign yourself to being unpopular. Even with your own mum! But I didn't mind. Mr Hennessy was going to rescue a dog; that was the main thing.

"And I should think," said Jilly, "that Dixie might still be there because most people would be too terrified to take on a pit bull."

"I wouldn't," I said.

"No," said Jilly, "but you're not normal."

"Neither are you!" I said.

"Never said I was. Wouldn't want to be," said Jilly. "Not if it means chucking animals out when you get a bit tired of them or can't be bothered with them any more. Not if it means *eating* them and *shooting* them and—"

"Hunting them," I said.

We both heaved big sighs. Never a day went by without us thinking of Foxglove. That same morning, taking Mud for his walk, we bumped into Darren. He asked us why we looked so glum and before we knew it we were pouring out the whole story. He may have seemed an odd person to confide in when you consider that he'd sided with Geraldine and old No-Neck on the subject of hunting, but we hadn't got the impression that he actually hated foxes or that he would have enjoyed watching them being torn to pieces.

When he heard about Foxglove he shuffled his feet and said that he was really sorry.

"It's kind of upsetting when things are killed."

"Do you think she would have been killed?" I said.

"Dunno," said Darren. "They ain't always." And then he shuffled a bit more and said, "I could try and find out, if you like."

"*Could* you?" I said. I thought that even if the news was bad, it would be a relief just to know.

"I could try," he said.

Next day he rang me up. I went all cold and

shivery when Mum said it was Darren on the phone. I just didn't know what I would do if he said that Foxglove had been killed. How would I ever manage to break the news to Jilly?

I picked up the receiver really cautiously, like it was covered in some kind of horrible slime.

"Did you – find out anything?" I whispered.

"Yeah, it's all right," said Darren. "They didn't have no kill."

"You mean – " my heart did a great springing leap – "you mean she got away?"

"I reckon," said Darren. "Any rate, they didn't kill nothing. They was all hopping mad 'cos it was the last hunt of the season. Don't have no more till cubbing starts."

I froze. I said, "*Cubbing?* What's that?"

"Oh. Well. You know!" I could tell, even over the phone, that Darren was embarrassed and wished he hadn't mentioned it.

"No, I don't!" I said. "Tell me!"

"Well, it's – when they, like ... train the dogs."

There was a silence.

"How?" I said.

Darren mumbled something.

"Train them *how*?" I screamed.

"On the cubs," said Darren. And then in a great rush, "I gotta go now, my mum's calling me."

"I just bet!" I said.

"No, she is, honest! I just thought you'd like to know about your one not being killed. I thought you'd be glad I found out for you."

Of course I was glad about Foxglove. If he hadn't told me about cubbing I'd have been over the moon. But I hadn't realized that those horrid, brutal beasts went out chasing cubs. It really upset me! Was there no end to the wicked things that people did?

When I told Jilly that Foxglove had got away she was so overjoyed she started dancing around with Mud, holding him by his front paws and doing a little jig and singing along with herself.

"Hooray, hooray! Foxglove got away!"

She couldn't understand why I was still dejected.

"What's the matter? Why are you being all flobby and miserable?"

So then I told her about the cubbing, and she stared at me as if she just couldn't believe it.

"They chase *cubs*? Tiny little *cubs*?"

"Darren said they t-train the dogs."

I thought for a minute that Jilly was going to run about and start smashing things. I felt really mean and almost wished I hadn't told her. Just seconds ago she'd been so happy, dancing and singing, and now here she was cast back into the deepest gloom.

The only solace we had was that at least Foxglove was safe.

At least, we thought she was.

Chapter 5

It was the last day of the Easter holidays. Mum was going to London to meet an old friend who was flying in from America. They hadn't seen each other since they were at college and Mum was in a right flap, wondering what to wear. She wanted to look

a) smart

but

b) casual

and

c) *young*.

What she didn't want to look was

a) dowdy

or

b) tarted up

or

c) mutton dressed as lamb.

I said, "What's mutton dressed as lamb?" and Mum said, "Like a middle-aged woman pretending to be a teenager... Oh! This is almost as bad as going out on my first date all over again!"

"It's only a *school* friend," I said.

Mum gave me a look.

"Just wear jeans," I said. "I would," and trundled downstairs to let Mud into the garden.

He'd only been out there a split second before he started barking. Mum yelled, "Clara! Make that dog be quiet!"

I went into the garden and said, "Mud, shut up!" I always talk to him, even though he can't hear. He was down by the back wall, barking his head off, so I grabbed him by his ruff and hauled him indoors before Mum could get ratty. She was quite ratty already on account of discovering that two of her favourite skirts would no longer do up. I told her that was because she'd been going out to dinner with Beastly Bernard too often, and she snapped, "That's got nothing to do with it! I'm just getting older."

Well! So am I, but I don't complain about it. I

said this to Mum and she retorted, "You wait till you get to my age!"

Does she truly believe that in twenty years' time I'll be wailing and moaning and gnashing my teeth all because I'm going to meet Geraldine Hooper and can't find anything to wear?

I don't think so!

When at last Mum had found some clothes that still fitted her and that weren't either too dowdy or too smart, or too young or too old, or too out of fashion or she didn't know why she'd bought them in the first place, I heaved a sigh of relief.

"I'm such a nuisance, aren't I?" she said. "I'll go in a minute. Where's my bag? Have you seen my bag? What have I done with the car keys? Wh—"

I rounded everything up for her, including Benjy, who was being dropped off at his little friend's in the village, thank goodness! It's a real drag if he's with me all day as I have to keep a constant eye on him.

"Now, are you sure you'll be all right?" said Mum.

"Yes," I said. "I'll be fine."

I was quite looking forward to a whole day all to myself, especially as it was the last one before school began again. Jilly and I had plans! We were going to make ourselves a picnic and take Mud and go on a long long hike, all across the fields.

"You're sure you wouldn't rather go with Benjy?" said Mum.

Horror of horrors! What an idea.

"Mum, I'm not a *baby*," I said.

"No, well, you know where to find me," said Mum. "I've left the number on the telephone table. I'll be back about five. Don't forget to get yourself something to eat. Oh, and Clara—"

"*Mum!*" I screamed. "I'll be all *right*!"

"Oh. Well ... all right." Mum gave a little laugh. "Have a nice day!"

"And you," I said.

The minute Mum had gone I flew into the back garden and called over the fence to Jilly.

"Are you ready?"

"Yes." Jilly's head popped out of her kitchen door. "I've done my bit of picnic. I'll bring it round."

Mud was barking at the wall again. I didn't know what his problem was but I couldn't be bothered to stop him. There wasn't anyone he could disturb. Jilly's mum was at work and Mrs Cherry is pretty deaf and I didn't think Mr Hennessy would mind. After all, he was a dog person!

Jilly came round and proudly showed me all the stuff she'd got for the picnic. Sausage rolls (veggie ones, natch!) a bag of crisps, a KitKat, two apples, some carrots (in case we came across a horse), a can of Coke and a plastic bottle full of water (for Mud, in case he got thirsty).

I said that I would pack some dog biscuits for him in case he got hungry.

"Why is he barking?" said Jilly.

I said, "I dunno. He's been doing it all morning. I stopped him once but he started again."

"He doesn't bark for no reason," said Jilly. "I'll go and look."

Seconds later she was back, pale and shaking at the kitchen door.

"Clara, come quick!" she said.

"Why? What is it?"

"Just *come*!" said Jilly.

I ran with her to the end of the garden. Mud was still there, still barking, leaping at the wall in a frenzy. Jilly pointed, with an unsteady finger.

"Over there."

I hoicked an arm round the branch of a nearby apple tree, braced one foot against the trunk and managed to heave myself up just far enough to peer over. There, amongst some leaves, was what looked like a bundle of old fur.

And then I saw that it wasn't just fur. It was a fox. A fox with a white tip to its tail...

I fell back to the ground. My heart was hammering, bang THUD, bang THUD! The roof of my mouth had gone dry.

"It's Foxglove, isn't it?" quavered Jilly. "She's dead, isn't she?"

"I don't know." I forked my hair back over my ears. My fingers were trembling, just like Jilly's had been, and my legs had gone all weak and wobblesome. I desperately didn't want to, but I knew that we had to be brave and go and investigate.

I said this to Jilly, and she pressed her lips very tightly together and nodded.

"We'll both go," I said.

Jilly nodded again. It was like she had lost the power of speech.

"I wish Mum was here!" The words came bursting out of me before I could stop them. Jilly shot me a scared look.

"I'm frightened!" I said.

Jilly swallowed. "So'm I."

But it had to be done. Foxglove could be injured and in pain. We had to go and check.

We shut Mud indoors and went out through the back gate. I have never in my life wanted so much to turn round and run. But Jilly kept going, and so I did as well. We gave each other courage.

And oh! We needed it. Our poor beautiful Foxglove must have been hit by a car. She had the most terrible gash down her flank. It was gaping wide – the lovely fur all matted and mangled, black with old, stale blood. Worst of all, it was churning with maggots. Fat, white, horrible maggots.

She lay there, her ears pulled back, her mouth stretched wide in a grimace of pain. Just lay there, staring up at us out of glazed eyes, too weak to move or defend herself.

Both of us knew that if a wild animal makes no attempt to flee from you, it means it's in a bad way. A really bad way. Our poor Foxglove hadn't even the energy to try and crawl into the undergrowth. She must have dragged herself as far as the garden, remembering perhaps the old days when she had been fit and strong and had sprung over the wall to find the food that we left for her. But she hadn't quite been able to make it. Her strength had given out and she had lain down to die.

"Oh, God!" said Jilly. "What do we do?"

"I don't know!"

I knelt down beside Foxglove. Even then she didn't pull away. I touched her, and a tremor ran through her. Her poor, clouded eyes that had once been so bright now seemed to be pleading: put me out of my misery!

I thought of the mouse and how I hadn't been brave enough to kill it. I had sworn then that next time I wouldn't flinch. But even if I could pluck up the courage, I wasn't sure that I would be strong enough to do it properly. "Quickly and cleanly". We needed someone like Beastly Bernard.

"Mr Hennessy!" I said. "Let's get Mr Hennessy!"

Jilly and I went charging back up the side of the house and into Honeypot Lane. Mr Hennessy lived in the first cottage. We tore up his garden path and banged and thumped on his front door. I prayed that he would be in.

"Please please please please!"

It seemed like ages before the door opened. Mr Hennessy stood there with a towel round his neck and a razor in his hand and his face all covered in shaving cream. He said, "Hallo, you two! What's the big disaster?"

"Foxglove," babbled Jilly.

"We think she's been run over—"

"She's in the lane—"

"She can't move!"

"Is she dead?" said Mr Hennessy.

I shook my head and tears went spurting in all directions.

"No, but we think she needs to be p-put out of her misery and we're not s-strong enough!"

"Hang on," said Mr Hennessy. He snatched at the towel and wiped the cream off his face. "Let me get a spade and I'll come and have a look."

Foxglove lay where we had left her. A pathetic heap of blood and bones and suffering. She barely turned her head as we approached.

"Does she—"

"Is she—"

We both stopped and tried again.

"Do you think we –"

– "have to –"

– "put her out of her misery?"

Unlike the Beast, Mr Hennessy hesitated. He set down the spade and squatted on his haunches, studying the poor mangled body of our beautiful Foxglove.

"I hate to kill an animal unless it's absolutely necessary. Her wound's obviously infected and she's certainly very sick, but I think it might be worth getting her to a vet. Do you know a vet?"

I said, "Yes! There's one in the village."

"Then let's get her there. Clara, you go and

ring the surgery and tell them we're bringing in an emergency. Jilly, you help me get her into the car. I'll bring it round as close as I can, then we'll try rolling her on to a blanket."

When I got back from ringing the vet, Jilly and Mr Hennessy were very gently lifting Foxglove into the back of Mr Hennessy's car. I saw that she had a bandage tied round her muzzle. Mr Hennessy caught me looking at it and said, "It's a necessary precaution. You should never take a chance with a wild animal."

I was just so relieved that he was there! Otherwise I don't know how we would have got Foxglove to the vet.

Our vet – Mud's vet! – is called Mr Johnson. Fortunately he is a very nice man who loves all animals including foxes and does not think of them as vermin or vicious killing machines. He told us to leave Foxglove with him and to ring back in an hour's time.

"Then I'll be able to tell you a bit more."

He meant that he would then be able to tell us whether it was worth trying to save her or whether he had had to put her down...

Jilly and I took Mud for a sad walk across the fields. No picnic. Mud couldn't understand why we didn't want to run and play with him as we usually did, but we were too full of sorrow. My heart hung like a great lump of lead inside me. Jilly said she thought that the bottom of her stomach had fallen out. I kept wailing, "If only I'd gone to look earlier, when Mud first started barking!"

"It's not your fault," said Jilly.

"It is!" I said. "*You* went to look!"

"Well." Jilly humped a shoulder. "It was only 'cos I had nothing else to do."

I refused to be comforted. I felt that it was all because of me that Foxglove had had to suffer longer than she should, and I moaned on and on about it till I expect Jilly probably felt like hitting me. *I* would have felt like hitting me. But Jilly was really generous. She said, "You were the one who thought of getting Mr Hennessy. We couldn't have done it without him."

Mr Hennessy had told us to call round at his place after Mud's walk and he would ring the vet while we were there. Jilly and I hovered at his elbow, trying to work out what was being said at the other end of the line.

Mr Hennessy said, "Yes. Right... Right. Sure! OK. Fine. Yup!" He stuck up a thumb. Jilly and I held our breath. "Will do," said Mr Hennessy. "Be with you in a few minutes."

"What's happened?"

"Is she going to be all right?"

Jilly and I spoke together.

"The vet thinks she stands a chance," said Mr Hennessy. "She's had all those ghastly maggots removed, the wound's been cleaned, and she's been given an antibiotic. There's also a fracture, which he's set. But that's as much as he can do. What she needs now is special nursing by someone who's experienced. Any ideas?"

We both immediately thought of Meg. We always think of Meg! But when we rang her she said regretfully that she had her hands far too full to take on a sick fox, much as she would like to.

"What you need is a proper wildlife hospital."

"Like St Tiggywinkle's?" I said.

Everyone has heard of St Tiggywinkle's! But

they are in Buckinghamshire, and that is miles away.

"There's a place over at Wandle Down," said Meg. "That's not too far. Why don't you try there? I can give you the number."

When I told Mr Hennessy he pulled ever such a funny face. He said, "Is that the only one?"

"It's the only one Meg told me about."

"And it is quite near," said Jilly.

"Oh, all right!" Mr Hennessy picked up his jacket. "If it has to be, it has to be. Come on! Let's go and pick up the invalid."

Now that I knew Foxglove had a chance, I immediately began to worry about who was going to pay the vet's bill. My family really doesn't have much money – Mum is for ever tearing her hair over those horrible things called Final Notices – and I just knew she would hit the roof if I asked her to pay for it. But to my great astonishment Mr Johnson told us that it was "on the house".

"You mean ... it's free?" I said. I couldn't believe it! "We don't have to pay?"

"Not for a wild life casualty," said Mr Johnson;

and he laughed, because I expect my amazement was showing in my face.

I learnt later that many vets will give their services free if you take wild animals in to them. I think that's really good. It shows that not everyone is as money-grubbing as you are led to believe. Jilly said that when she became a vet (which is what she hopes to be) she would always treat wild animals for nothing.

"And stray dogs and cats. And if people are too poor or are old age pensioners."

Mr Hennessy laughed and said, "You sound as if you're going to be a charity!"

"Well, perhaps I will be," said Jilly. "I don't really want to make money. Just help animals."

When he heard that we were taking Foxglove to a wildlife hospital, Mr Johnson very kindly lent us a carrying cage specially designed for foxes.

"I think she's too knocked out to give you any problems, but better safe than sorry."

Poor Foxglove! She was just a small, limp bundle in her carrying cage. She looked so desperately ill that I couldn't believe she would ever be well and strong again, but Mr Johnson said that he'd seen worse cases recover.

"And be released back into the wild. It all depends on the quality of the nursing."

"The quality of the nursing," said Mr Hennessy, "will be excellent."

We wondered how he knew.

"Well!" he said. "It always is. The people who run these places are animal mad."

"Like us," said Jilly.

I was worried in case they might not have room for Foxglove. I thought we ought to ring and check. Mr Hennessy said, "They'll have room. But I'll give them a ring, if you like, just to tell them we're coming. You two stay here in the car, I'll nip back inside and give them a call."

We watched him go.

"He didn't take the number," I said.

"What number?" said Jilly.

"Number of the hospital. I've still got it here."

"Oh?"

Jilly didn't seem very interested in Mr Hennessy not having the number. I said, "How can he ring if he hasn't got the number?"

"They've probably got it in the vet's," said Jilly. And then, in a big rush, she said, "If ever I was going to get married, which of course I'm *not*," she added hastily, since we'd already agreed we thought that husbands on the whole were just a nuisance, "but if ever I *did*, then it would be to someone like Mr Hennessy. He's such a darling!"

"Unlike Beastly Bernard," I said. I had just looked back at Foxglove, lying in her cage, and it had occurred to me that if the Beast had been there and we'd run to him for help, he'd have picked up a spade and bashed poor Foxglove's head in just like he'd bashed the mouse. And Mum would have said, "It was the kindest thing," and Jilly and I would have wept buckets but would have sadly agreed with her, because how were we to know any different? It was only thanks to Mr Hennessy that her life had been spared and that she stood a chance of getting better.

"I wish Mum would give Beastly B. the elbow and fall for Mr Hennessy instead," I said.

"Yes! That would be brilliant," said Jilly. "Then they could get married and he'd be your stepdad."

"Hm ... not a bad idea!" I said.

"We'd share him, though, wouldn't we?" said Jilly.

She sounded quite anxious about it!

I said, "I have never actually *heard* of anyone sharing their stepdad with their best friend, but I suppose I might."

"We'll work on it!" said Jilly.

We felt a bit guilty when Mr Hennessy came back to the car.

"What are you two giggling about?" he said.

"Oh, nothing," I said, airily. "Did you ring them? You didn't take the number."

"I found it," he said.

"Is it all right?"

"Of course it is! I told you it would be. Are you OK back there, Jilly?"

Jilly nodded, blissfully. I was up front with Mr Hennessy, and she was at the back with Foxglove, keeping a watchful eye on the cage.

"Right!" Mr Hennessy slammed his door shut. "Let's hit the road!"

Chapter 6

The wild animal hospital wasn't at all what I'd expected. I'd imagined it as being a bit like an ordinary human hospital, except with animals for patients. Which is stupid, really, when you stop and think about it. Wild animals need dark little corners where they can burrow away and keep out of sight of human beings. They wouldn't be at all happy in a busy ward with lots of bright lights and nowhere to hide.

Even the outside didn't look much like a hospital. In fact, it didn't look anything like a hospital. It looked more like a – well! Just a messy bit of farmyard with an old ramshackle building in one corner and a pond in the middle. The pond was surrounded by wire mesh and there were lots of ducks and geese paddling about in it.

There was also a pen with a couple of rabbits, and a big van with the words WANDLE DOWN WILDLIFE HOSPITAL painted on one side. If it hadn't been for the van I might almost have thought we'd come to the wrong place. How could you have a hospital in a farmyard?

Jilly was obviously just as puzzled as I was.

"Is this it?" she said.

"Yup!" Mr Hennessy switched off the engine. "This is it. You stay here, I'll go and find someone."

We watched Mr Hennessy go striding off across the yard.

"I hope it's going to be all right," said Jilly.

"It is! They said."

"No, I mean—" She leaned forward and waved a hand. "It just looks so mucky!"

I knew what she meant. I stared doubtfully at the duck-pond with its makeshift netting. I looked at all the puddles and the muddy grass and the tumbledown building. Could this truly be a *hospital*?

And then Mr Hennessy came back accompanied by a blonde woman who was just so incredibly and amazingly beautiful that she might have been a model. Even dressed in old raggedy jeans and a grubby sweatshirt she looked like she had just stepped off the catwalk. Extraordinary! Jilly and I couldn't stop staring.

Mr Hennessy said, "Girls, this is Angel. She runs the place. Angel, meet Jilly and Clara. They're the ones who found the fox. They're animal fanatics, aren't you, girls?"

We agreed that we were.

"Glad to hear it," said Angel. She had a very light, clear voice. Rather brisk, like a headmistress I once had. "Let's get the patient settled." She looked at Mr Hennessy. "I'll need you to give me a hand."

"Yes, of course," said Mr Hennessy.

Between them they lifted Foxglove, in her cage, out of the car, carried her across the yard and into the ramshackle building. Jilly and I made to follow, but quite sharply, over her shoulder, Angel said, "I'd rather you stayed out here, if you don't mind. You can have a look round in a minute. The patient's my priority right now."

Jilly flushed, and I think I did a bit, as well.

"She's our fox," muttered Jilly. "Why can't we go with her?"

It seemed so unfair! It was also worrying, because how did we know where this woman was taking her?

We wandered over to the pond to look at the ducks and the geese. They seemed quite happy, in spite of being kept in a wire netting enclosure. Some of them were in the water, bobbing up and down like corks or just idly paddling around. Others were plopping about on the grass, pecking at worms or sometimes at the wire netting. When we looked more closely we could see that several of them had obviously had accidents because there was one with a crumpled wing, a couple with only one leg, one which had an eye missing and one with a damaged beak.

"All casualties," said a voice from behind us. We turned, and there was this girl standing there. She was wearing jeans and wellies and obviously worked at the hospital, or at any rate helped out. I was dead envious because she didn't look all that much older than me and Jilly, and I would have loved to be able to nurse wild animals and see them get better.

The girl told us how some of the ducks and geese had been attacked by dogs and that some were road accidents. The one with only one eye had been shot at with an air pistol, and the one with a crumpled wing had been found by a member of the public.

"They always come to us if they find anything. We've only been open a few months but we're getting to be really well known in the area. You name it, we've got it! Are you the ones who brought the fox in?"

We nodded.

"Well, you've brought it to the right place! Angel's the best. She's absolutely brilliant with animals."

The girl went off across the yard and disappeared into the ramshackle building where Foxglove had been taken. Her words had reassured us slightly, though we still didn't see why we couldn't have gone with Mr Hennessy.

"We were the ones who found her," grumbled Jilly.

"I know," I said. I resented being treated like someone who was too young to be told what was going on. Foxglove wasn't the first animal we'd rescued. We weren't total beginners!

Mr Hennessy was coming back across the yard, with the Angel woman. We studied their faces anxiously, trying to decide if the news was good or bad.

"Well! It's a nasty wound and she's got a raging infection," said Angel. "She must have been hit some days ago. They carry on as long as they can, but in the end it defeats them. She'd certainly have died if you hadn't found her."

"Will she get better?" I said.

"Should do. Might be a long job, but we'll get her on her feet again. Send her back where she came from. Actually, I think I had a call about this one. Easter Sunday. Someone rang in from your neck of the woods. Said they'd seen a fox hit by a car. Said she looked exhausted, as if she was at the end of her tether. Had a white tip to her tail. Should think it's the same one."

Easter Sunday! Jilly and I exchanged glances.

"That was the day of the hunt," I said; and I

told Angel how we'd been taking Mud for his walk and how the hunt had suddenly come thundering down on us. "And it was Foxglove!" I said. "They were after her."

"That would account for it. She was obviously stressed out. Completely done in. Hit by a car. It figures."

"Do you approve of fox hunting?" I said, timidly.

Mr Hennessy gave a short laugh. Angel flashed him this really filthy look. She snapped, "Approve? I'd shoot the so-and-so's if I had my way!"

"Sh-shoot the foxes?" I stammered.

This time I thought Mr Hennessy would choke himself, he laughed so much.

"Not the foxes." Angel said it scathingly. "The brutes who hunt them. Don't ever let anyone tell you it's necessary. It's not. They hunt because they enjoy it. Then they have to try and find an excuse for themselves. And so you get these horror stories of foxes being killers, of foxes taking lambs—"

"Don't they?" said Jilly. Quite bravely, I

thought. I wouldn't have dared interrupt this woman! She was really fierce. "Don't they take lambs?"

"The odd one or two. Why shouldn't they? They have to eat. But they only take what they need; they're not like human beings. They don't eat for the sake of eating. And for your information, most of the lambs taken by foxes are either already dead or else they're sick and not likely to survive anyway. If you don't believe me, look up the figures! Even the Ministry of Agriculture doesn't regard them as a significant threat. In fact any sensible farmer would look upon the fox as his friend. They eat rabbits and they eat mice. What do people want to kill them for? Because they've got a blood lust, that's why! Utterly despicable."

"Phew!" Mr Hennessy wiped the back of his hand across his forehead. "That's told you!"

"If they didn't want to know," said Angel, "they shouldn't have asked."

"We did want to know." Jilly said it earnestly. "We've been having these arguments with people at school and we didn't know what to say."

"Well, now you do. You can tell them. Foxes are not a pest and there is no excuse for hunting them."

"We don't think there's an excuse for hunting any animal," said Jilly.

"Quite right. Come and have a look round. I'm sorry I couldn't let you into the actual hospital, but it stresses the patients if too many people go traipsing in and out. They like to be private. But you're welcome to come and see some of the ones that are on the mend." She looked at Mr Hennessy. "Are you coming with us, or not?"

"Er – no. That's all right. I'll stay here and talk to the ducks."

"Just as you like. Come along, then, you two!"

She strode off and we meekly hustled after her, down by the side of the ramshackle building and into what must once have been someone's garden. Now it was full of sheds and shacks and animal pens.

Angel took us into one of the sheds. A strong smell of fox hit us immediately.

"This is Ruby," she said.

A foxy face peered at us, suspiciously, from

out of a den that she had made for herself at the back of a large cage.

"Ruby was our very first patient. She was brought in as a road accident. Both her back legs were useless. She'd been dragging herself round on her front ones, and in the end they'd given up on her, as well."

"Oh! That's terrible!" said Jilly. "How did she manage to survive?"

"She nearly didn't is the answer to that. Couldn't move fast enough to catch anything. She was near to starvation when she came to us. Now she's almost ready to go outside and join some of the others."

"Then will she be able to be released?" said Jilly.

"No. Never. We'll have to find a sanctuary that can take her in."

"But she will be able to walk?"

"In time. It would be cruel to keep her alive if she couldn't walk. But she's been too damaged to get by out there on her own. Come and see Arthur."

Arthur was a dog fox, and he was *big*. He really was the size of a German Shepherd.

He was outside, in a pen, sunning himself. He looked up at us and stretched his mouth in a great yawn, but didn't bother to move away.

"He's one of our permanent residents," said Angel. "He's a very old boy, he can't get around too well any more. Got a touch of arthritis, haven't you, my lovey?"

"How did he get here?" asked Jilly.

"He used to visit someone's garden. They used to feed him. Probably kept him going. Then one day they noticed he was getting a bit stiff, couldn't walk too well, so they called us in and now at least he's ending his days in comfort."

"That's really nice," said Jilly.

"I think so."

"It's like he's come to a sort of animal rest home. Like Mr Woodvine," said Jilly. "He's gone to sheltered accommodation."

I couldn't really imagine that this alarming woman would be in the least bit interested in Mr Woodvine, but to my surprise she nodded and said, "Yes. If we can have sheltered accommodation for elderly human beings, why shouldn't we have it for animals? Come and say hallo to Bonny. Who wasn't at all bonny when she came to us. Were you, my pretty?"

Bonny *was* pretty. A little vixen, almost as beautiful as Foxglove. Her sharp pointy face peered anxiously out at us from behind a bale of straw.

"She was at death's door," said Angel. "Just a bag of skin and bone, covered in mange. She'd crawled into someone's garage to die. The first few days I honestly thought it might be kinder to put an end to her. But she pulled through. She'll be due for release in a week or two. Don't ever believe that you can't treat foxes for mange! You can. I've proved it."

Jilly said yes, we had read about foxes and mange.

"In an animal magazine. We try to read as much as we can. We belong to this organization called Animal Lovers."

She pointed to her badge with its slogan, We Love Animals. We always wear our badges, wherever we go. Angel glanced at it and nodded.

"Good!" she said. "There's nothing like hands-on experience – we all have to start somewhere. Kate, the girl you met, comes and helps out whenever she can. It's valuable experience for her. She's going to be a vet."

"That's what I'm going to be!" said Jilly.

"I'm going to run an animal sanctuary," I said; but Angel had already moved on and I don't think she heard me. I felt a bit forlorn and left out because she and Jilly seemed to be getting on really well.

After the foxes we saw some badgers, including one poor little torn one that had been set on by hideous yobs with dogs, and another that had been caught in a snare and almost strangled.

"Ghastly things!" said Angel. "People ought to be shot."

Jilly made a noise that sounded suspiciously like a giggle that has hastily been turned into a hiccup. I suppose it was kind of funny the way someone with the name Angel kept on about shooting people. But I agreed with her!

Well, maybe I don't agree that they should be *shot*, because I don't believe in guns. Maybe what should happen is, they should be trapped in their own snares, or set on by man-eating sharks, or chased by people on horseback until they dropped with exhaustion. *That* would teach them.

As well as the foxes and badgers there were some gorgeous beautiful owls and a swan that had got tangled up in a discarded fishing line ("The things are a menace!" said Angel) and lots and lots of little hedgehogs.

We were just about to go back to the car when Jilly said, "*Oh!* Fox cubs!"

"Oh, yes. I almost forgot. That's our nursery," said Angel.

Jilly and I watched, enchanted, as half a dozen tiny baby fox cubs tumbled and rolled in their pen. At the back of the pen was a barrier they could hide behind if they felt shy. One of them did, and kept peeping out at us! But the others just went right on playing as if we didn't exist.

We would have loved to pick them up and cuddle them, but we'd learnt enough to know that that was something you shouldn't do. Angel would really have jumped on us if we'd suggested it! It is a terrible temptation because fox cubs are really sweet, but it would be dangerous for them to become too trusting of human beings. So we contented ourselves with just watching them and marvelling at the fact that we were seeing real live fox cubs at play. Not on television, but right there in front of us!

Jilly, who seemed to be better at talking to Angel than I was, said sadly that she supposed if Foxglove had had any cubs they would have died by now.

Angel said, "Why?"

All abruptly, just like that. It really put me off! But Jilly stood her ground. She said, "Well, they wouldn't have been weaned."

"Why not?" said Angel. "It all depends when they were born and whether she's managed to go on feeding them the last ten days. If she has, then they'll probably just about be on to solids. They might well have survived."

I surprised myself by blurting out, "So long as they don't get killed when cubbing starts!"

A great angry flare of colour came into Angel's cheeks. She snarled, "Don't talk to me about that disgraceful practice! Anyone who trains dogs to tear young animals to pieces deserves to be hanged, drawn and quartered!"

Which I think must be even worse than being shot!

As we left we thanked her for taking Foxglove. She said, "Not at all. That's what I'm here for." And then she softened a bit and said, "Thank *you* for taking the trouble to bring her in."

"It's what we do," said Jilly. "We've dedicated our lives to rescuing animals."

"Well, you know where to find us if you rescue any more."

"When Foxglove is ready to be released –" I said it rather nervously, expecting to be snapped or snarled at – "could we come and see her again?"

To my great surprise and joy Angel didn't snap or snarl but said, "By all means! You can come and help us release her, if you like."

"Oh!" I felt my cheeks go crimson. I couldn't think of a single word to say. It was just something that was so completely and utterly unexpected.

"I wouldn't let just anybody," said Angel. And

then she smiled. She actually smiled! And my heart just turned right over and I went all sort of melty inside. At last I had won her approval!

"I suppose now you'll be wanting a donation," said Mr Hennessy.

Angel looked at him, rather haughtily. "That's entirely up to you."

Jilly cried, "I've got some money!" and turned out her jeans pocket and came up with just under £3. I, unfortunately didn't have anything. But Mr Hennessy told Jilly to put it away again. He said, "It's all right, I'm only kidding. I'll give a cheque."

"Gratefully received," said Angel.

"Don't mention it," said Mr Hennessy.

I had the feeling that he had taken against her. I was anxious to explain to him how sometimes people could be good with animals but a bit awkward with human beings, but as soon as we had piled into the car (with me sitting at the back this time) Jilly started chattering. All about how maybe Mr Hennessy should have taken Foxglove back to his place and looked after her there.

"And then we could have helped you and you could have written a book about it."

Mr Hennessy said it was a nice idea but that he was afraid he was a bit too squeamish.

"I can't stand the sight of blood."

"You didn't mind it this morning, when we picked her up," said Jilly.

"Ah, well! You rise to the occasion, don't you? You do what has to be done. That was an emergency. But in any case –" he half turned and gave an apologetic grin – "I don't think I could stand the smell!"

It was true that there had been a great smell of fox and badger and other creatures at the wildlife hospital, but it wasn't really unpleasant and I felt sure you would quite quickly get used to it.

"Maybe if you're really dedicated," said Mr Hennessy.

I listened to him and Jilly chatting together, and I started weaving this blissful daydream in which Mum and Mr Hennessy got married and we all moved to a house in the middle of a field. Mum would do her translating (which is how she earns her living) and Mr Hennessy would write his articles, and in our spare time we would rescue wild creatures. And ones that weren't wild, too. We would still live in Riddlestone, and I would still be best friends with Jilly, and every weekend she would come and stay with us and help look after all the animals. And Mr Hennessy would get used to the smell, and the sight of blood, and Mum would stop worrying about Final Notices because we would turn ourselves into a charity and people would send us donations for all the good and useful work that we were doing.

It was a beautiful daydream, so you can imagine what a shock it was when I swam back to reality and heard the following bit of conversation:

Jilly: "Angel is so lovely, isn't she?"

Mr Hennessy: "Yes. Lovely."

Jilly: "Do you think that's really her name? Angel?"

Mr Hennessy: "No. Her real name is Angela."

Jilly: (Surprised) "Oh! Do you know her?"

Mr Hennessy: "She's my wife."

Well! That was my daydream shattered. Or so I thought.

"Perhaps I should have said my soon-to-be-ex-wife," said Mr Hennessy. He pulled down the corners of his mouth. "We're in the middle of getting divorced."

Three cheers! I nearly bounced on the back seat with joy.

"I'm sorry," said Mr Hennessy. "I should have told you earlier. It's why I originally tried to wriggle out of coming here."

"That's all right." Jilly said it kindly. "We understand. My mum and dad are divorced. So are Clara's. Lots of people are."

"But it's always horrid," I said, remembering how I'd cried when Dad had left home.

"It's sad," agreed Mr Hennessy. "But sometimes people just grow apart. If I make a confession, will you promise not to hate me for ever?"

We solemnly promised.

"It was Angel's obsession with animals that finally came between us. I do like animals! I'd never do anything to harm one. But I'm not prepared to devote my life to them 100 per cent the way she does. Where animals are concerned,

Angel truly *is* an angel. Your Foxglove will be quite safe with her. But where people are concerned – well! Let's just say she's not so good."

I think perhaps that I may be like that. I don't know for sure, but quite often I find myself very out of sympathy with people. The sort of people who set dogs on to badgers, or catch fish with hooks, or lay snares, or hunt foxes, or shoot birds, or – oh! The list is endless.

I never feel out of sympathy with animals.

"I suppose you'll now despise me utterly," said Mr Hennessy, "and decide that I am not worth knowing."

"Oh, no! We are quite broad minded," said Jilly. "We realize that not everybody can live the way that people like Meg and Angel live. And the way that we will live," she added, "once we're grown up."

"That's right," I said, eager to reassure him. "Our mums couldn't, for instance. My mum is fond of animals but in what she calls *moderation*."

"I guess I'm like that," said Mr Hennessy.

I sat beaming to myself in the back seat (which still smelt nice and foxy). I was feeling happier than I had in days. We'd rescued Foxglove and earned the respect of a very wonderful woman and Mr Hennessy could still become my stepdad.

It was all working out really well!

Chapter 7

We would have loved to go and visit Foxglove and see how she was doing, but we were scared that we would just be a nuisance and get in the way. We were also worried that we would waste people's time when they could be doing more valuable things, such as looking after the animals. In any case, Angel probably wouldn't have let us go and talk to Foxglove as she would say that it was causing her stress. It seemed hard when she was our very own little fox that had come into our garden and that we had rescued, but as Jilly said, you couldn't ever really claim a wild animal as "yours".

"They have to be free and independent."

We agreed that you would need to be a very special sort of person to run a wildlife hospital.

With cats and dogs, you can have a real relationship. You can get to know them and talk to them and have a cuddle with them. But with wildlife you can't afford to do that, at least not if they are going to be released back into the wild. You have to keep your distance and make sure they don't become dependent on you. And you certainly can't ever cuddle them.

I said soberly to Jilly that although I would love to help look after wild creatures, I unfortunately didn't think I could bear not being able to get friendly with them.

Jilly said she didn't think she could bear it, either.

"But it will be different for you," I said, "because you're going to be a vet. All you'll have to do is just treat their injuries and say what medicine they're to have, and then they'll go off to be nursed by someone like Angel."

"That's true," admitted Jilly. "But I don't just want to treat animals and never get to know them!"

We decided that what we'd do was, we'd run a sanctuary that took in all kinds of creatures: dogs and cats, donkeys and horses, foxes and badgers, ducks and geese, and just everything that wasn't able to be re-homed or sent back to the wild.

"Like we'd take Arthur, 'cos he's old, and Ruby 'cos she can't ever look after herself again. And then it wouldn't matter if they got to know us."

"Yes, and I'll be a vet like Mr Johnson," said Jilly, "but I'll live at the sanctuary and all the money I earn will go to keep the animals."

"I wonder how you *get* a sanctuary?" I said.

Next time we went to help out at End of the Line we put this question to Meg. She said, "Now you're asking! Well, first off, you need some money. Winning the lottery would be a good idea. Failing that, you inherit a fortune from a relative. Do you have any relatives who are likely to leave you a fortune?"

Slowly, we shook our heads.

"I didn't, either," said Meg. "It makes life extremely difficult. I was like you. I had always wanted to help animals. So for a while I worked in rescue centres: Battersea Dogs' Home, Blue Cross. Didn't earn much, but loved the work.

Then I got married and we bought a house. Then I got divorced because my husband lost patience with me crowding the place out with animals that no one else wanted. You know ... old dogs that were going to be put down. Three-legged cats. One-eyed rabbits. That sort of thing. We put the house up for sale and with my half of the proceeds I bought this bungalow – which to be honest is little more than a shack. But the field came with it, and that was what I really wanted. I've been here for nearly ten years and I don't regret a day of it. So! Has that been of any help?"

We looked at each other.

"Do you mean, we have to get married?" said Jilly.

Meg laughed. "Would it be so awful? Who knows? You might find husbands who are as animal crazy as you are!"

"But they can be such a nuisance," I said. We were always hearing these stories about husbands who got mad at their wives for adopting too many animals or letting the dogs get into bed with them.

"Well, if you want to strike out and be

independent," said Meg, "the best thing to do would be to get yourselves what I call a Proper Paid job and earn enough money to buy a place of your own. That's what I would aim at."

I felt a bit glum when she said this. I don't want a Proper Paid job! Not if it means being in someone's beastly office or shop. I just want to help animals.

I wailed to Mum about it when I got home.

"What am I going to do? I'm not clever enough to be a vet and Meg says that other animal jobs don't pay enough money!"

"Enough money for what?" said Mum.

"For me to buy a field!"

"Oh. I see. You definitely want a field?"

"I've got to have one! For all the animals! And how am I going to get one if I haven't any money?"

"Nothing comes easy," said Mum, with a little sigh. "Most of us have to work for the things we want."

"I wish I had a rich nan who'd leave me a fortune!"

"If wishes were horses, beggars would ride.

I'm afraid it's no use wishing, Clara. You have to get out there and go for it."

"How?" I said, resentfully.

"Well, you're not going to like it but all I can suggest is that you concentrate hard on your school work, no more moaning and groaning, try to get yourself some good exam results and go to college."

"That's not helping with animals!"

"No, but it might just help you find a job that would pay enough for this field you're so desperate to have. You have to make an effort, you know. Nothing is going to fall into your lap."

I glared at her. I felt sure she was only saying it as a mean and underhand way of getting me to do my homework properly and not skimp.

"Jilly's going to have to work pretty hard," said Mum, "if she wants to be a vet. You wouldn't want to be left behind, would you?"

I humped a shoulder. "S'pose not."

"Well, there you are, then. Get on with it!" Briskly, Mum cleared a space on the table. "First week back at school, you must have plenty of homework to do."

124

I *knew* it was a trick. I can read Mum like a book! But all the same, it did make me think. Up until now, buying a field and a sanctuary had just been a beautiful daydream. Thanks to Mum – and to Meg – it was starting to become a real, serious ambition.

At school we told Darren about Foxglove and he must have told other people because lots of kids came up to us and said how they thought fox hunting was cruel and ought to be banned. Then our teacher got to hear of it and said that if we liked, we could organize a proper debate on the subject, as it would teach us how to speak in public and put our views across. So that was what we did. Jilly and me spoke against, and Geraldine and No-Neck spoke for. Then we had "questions from the floor" and people asked about foxes stealing lambs and getting into hen-runs, and we were able to tell them what Angel had said, and Jim at Hen Haven. After that we had a vote and you'll never guess ... the vote went to us by 29 to 3! Some victory!

Only two people didn't vote. One of them was Darren, who said he hadn't been able to make up his mind. However, as Jilly pointed out, even that was better than last term when he'd told us he thought fox hunting was necessary.

"At least now he's not so sure."

Meanwhile the poor pit bull, Dixie, was still at End of the Line. We hadn't given up hope that Mr Hennessy would come and rescue her, but he was away at the moment, on business. It was so sad, because she was starting to grow really dejected. She perked up a bit when we took her into the field to play, but drooped as soon as we led her back to her cage. She so much wanted to stay with us and have fun!

"If only Mr Hennessy were here," I sighed, as Jilly and me took Mud for his walk one Saturday morning. "I'd go and *beg* him."

"Yes, and if he were here," said Jilly, "he might take us to the Wildlife Hospital to see Foxglove. She must be in an outside pen by now, so I don't think Angel would mind us looking at her."

We did so want to see Foxglove again! We couldn't help thinking of her as ours and feeling responsible for her. I kept remembering her as she was when we had found her – that terrible mangled heap of blood and fur. I kept remembering how glazed her eyes had been, how she had pulled her lips back over her teeth with pain. I needed to know that she was all right!

Desperately we tried thinking up excuses that would take us back, such as an injured bird or an orphaned fox. But search as we might, we couldn't find any. Not a single one! It was Mud, in the end, who gave us the excuse we needed.

We were on our way back from the walk, carefully treading round the edge of a ploughed field, when quite suddenly Mud lit out. He went streaking across the diagonal, straight as an arrow, bounding over all the ridges and furrows as if they simply didn't exist. Jilly and I could only stand helplessly and watch.

"He must have seen something," said Jilly.

We thought it was probably a rabbit, and that he would come back when he had lost its scent.

Slowly we went on picking our way round the narrow shelf that was as much as the measly farmer had left for people to walk on.

"It's a right of way," grumbled Jilly. "There's a *stile*."

She's quite militant about these things. I am as well, a little bit, though not as much as Jilly. Once we came across a sign post that a farmer had deliberately turned the wrong way and Jilly insisted that we turn it back again. Another time she made me walk through a field of corn because there was a right of way there and the farmer had tried to get rid of it. I was terrified we would be shot for trespassing, but Jilly said we had to do it and, if we got shot, it would all be in a good cause. As if that made it OK!

As we battled along through beds of stinging nettles and horrid snatchy brambles, we kept our eye on Mud. By now he had reached the wire netting which separated the field from the golf course.

"Now what's he doing?" said Jilly, as Mud dived into the hedge.

We saw his rear end sticking out, tail frantically wagging. Then we heard him bark.

"That's his come-and-look-bark," I said.

So long as he was barking, there wasn't any problem. It was when he stopped barking you had to worry, because that meant he was concentrating all his energies on doing something else, such as—

"What's that?" I said.

We listened. We heard a high-pitched squealing, as if a small animal was being terrorized.

"Quick!" shrieked Jilly.

We ran just as fast as we could over that field, but we weren't as nimble as Mud. We kept slipping and stumbling and ricking our ankles. Ploughed fields are a real obstacle course. If Mud had caught something, there was just no way we were going to get there in time to stop him doing whatever it was he was doing.

"He wouldn't mean to kill!" I panted.

But if it was a really tiny little creature, like a shrew or a vole, say, he might try picking it up and could ever so easily kill it by mistake. I think both Jilly and me were dreading what we might be going to find.

The squealing, meanwhile, went on.

"Eeeeeeek! Eeeeeeek! Eeeeeeek!"

"It's a squirrel!" cried Jilly. "He's got a squirrel!"

Mud had it penned in a corner. It must have tried to run away from him and got itself caught under the wire netting. Its front half was one side, its back half the other. And Mud was—

Busily licking its bum!

We couldn't help giggling. Jilly held Mud while I prised up the netting for the squirrel to get through. It was then we saw that it was dragging one of its back legs. The poor little thing could hardly walk, which must have been why it had tried squeezing under the netting rather than shinning up a tree.

"Oh! Now what do we do?" said Jilly.

"Rescue it!" I said.

"How?"

I wasn't sure how, but I knew that it would die if we left it like that. Another dog would come along, and this one might not be as kind as Mud.

"We can't just abandon it," I said. "It looks like it's only a baby."

"It can still bite!" said Jilly.

"Mm." I furrowed my brow, trying to work out a plan. "Maybe one of us should stay here and guard it, while the other takes Mud home and –

and borrows a pair of your mum's gardening gloves!"

That way we could pick it up without getting bitten.

"And we'll need a box, as well, only not cardboard 'cos it could chew its way out."

"I'll find something," promised Jilly.

I hadn't necessarily meant for her to be the one to go and me to be the one left on guard, but as it was her mum's gloves that we wanted to borrow I couldn't very well object.

Jilly put Mud on his lead and dragged him off, and I settled down to wait.

It is incredibly boring, just waiting. Time seems to go on for ever. Nobody came by, either with or without a dog. The squirrel, fortunately, wasn't going anywhere. It just lay on its side, amongst some leaves, looking pathetic. I knew it was still alive because I could see it breathing, and when I tried talking to it it turned its head and looked at me out of its small bright squirrelly eyes.

People say that squirrels are like rats and that they're pests and vermin and ought to be killed, but I don't agree with going round killing things. Not even rats, unless you positively, absolutely have to. Rats, as a matter of fact, are highly intelligent and resourceful creatures and you can keep them as pets, though sadly they don't live for very long and I wouldn't like that.

Oh, dear! I could have sworn that a whole hour had passed before Jilly reappeared on the horizon, though she assured me it was no more than twenty minutes and that she had run all the way there and all the way back.

"What's that?" I said, pointing.

"Bread bin." Jilly held it out, proudly. "I thought it would do as a carrying box. It's got air holes, and look!" She opened it. "I've put some newspaper inside."

I had to admit that it was a brilliant idea.

"But what's your mum going to say?"

"She won't know." Jilly waved a hand, airily. "By the time she gets back" (Jilly's mum works in an antiques shop in the village) "the bread'll be back in there."

Well! We'd got the gloves and we'd got the carrying box. Now all we had to do was get the squirrel – only this time we didn't have Mr Hennessy to help us. We were going to have to do it by ourselves.

First of all we had to climb over the wire netting, and *that* wasn't easy. I ripped a huge great hole in my T-shirt and Jilly got one of her trainers stuck and had to undo the lace and take her foot out. Then we had to pick the squirrel up. We didn't want to hurt it more than it had already been hurt, but we didn't want it to hurt us, either. Squirrel bites can be really nasty.

"You hold the bread bin, I'll put him in there," I said.

You have to be firm when you're handling a wild animal. Not firm enough to squash it, but firm enough to stop it wriggling out of your grasp. I knew this, but it was the first time I'd ever attempted to do it and I was a bit nervous. In the end I just took a deep breath, scooped up the squirrel with both hands and thrust it into the bread bin. Jilly clapped down the shutter, and that was that. We'd captured a squirrel!

"Now what do we do?" said Jilly.

"Get Mum to take us to Wandle Down!" I said.

We headed home as fast as we could, but taking care not to jolt the poor squirrel too much. We found Mum in the back garden, clutching a pair of shears and staring dementedly at the thing she calls a lawn (but which in reality is just a patch of weedy grass and dandelions). At the moment it was looking a bit like a jungle.

"What have you got there?" said Mum.

When we told her it was an injured squirrel and we wanted to take it to the wildlife hospital she threw down the shears immediately and said, "I see! And I suppose you want me to drive you? Well, in that case I shall leave the grass for you."

"That's all right," I said. "We don't mind."

We hauled Benjy away from his computer game, shut Mud in the house and all bundled into the car. Benjy was excited because we'd told him about the fox cubs, we were excited because we hoped we'd see Foxglove, and Mum – well, Mum was just glad of any excuse not to cut the grass! She's not at all a gardening sort of person.

"But are you sure they'll take a squirrel?" she said. "There are some people round here who shoot them."

"Angel isn't like that," I assured her. "She's an animal person."

"Yes! She shoots people," said Jilly, and we both giggled.

It was really funny, because when we got there and Mum said to Angel about people shooting squirrels, Angel immediately said, "Yes, and I'd shoot *them* if I caught them at it!"

Needless to say, this set us off giggling again.

"What's so funny?" said Angel, rather sharply.

Between giggles I managed to explain how Mum had thought maybe she wouldn't take a squirrel as a patient.

"Nonsense!" snapped Angel. "Take any animal!"

I think Mum felt a bit rebuked. It was how I had felt, that first time, when Jilly and me had been told to stay behind while Angel and Mr Hennessy took Foxglove into the hospital.

"She's quite nice really," I whispered, as Angel went off with the squirrel in its bread bin.

"You could have fooled me," said Mum.

While we waited for Angel to come back we took Benjy to see the fox cubs. Mum kept wrinkling her nose because of the wild animal smell, but as I told her, we probably smelt just as bad to them.

"Even worse," said Jilly.

"Even worse," I agreed. After all, an animal's sense of smell is hugely superior to ours. "They probably think we *stink*," I said.

When Angel came back (with Jilly's mum's bread bin) we asked anxiously after both of our patients, the squirrel and Foxglove. Angel said that the squirrel would be fine and that Foxglove was doing well.

"Do you want to come and see her?"

We nodded, beaming, and she took us into the shed where Ruby used to be. Ruby, with Arthur, had now gone to a sanctuary to live out the rest of her days in peace and comfort, and it was our little Foxglove who was crouched in a heap of straw, watchfully glinting at us. She looked so much better! Her eyes were bright, her coat gleaming, and the terrible gash in her flank was almost healed.

We talked to her, hoping she might recognize the sound of our voices, or even our smell, but she wouldn't come close.

"Quite right," said Angel. "Keep as far away from human beings as possible. That's what I would do if I were a fox."

It was sad she didn't remember that we were the people who had rescued her, but you can't expect animals to be grateful. Angel said briskly that just seeing them happy and well again had to be reward enough.

"Another couple of weeks and she'll be fit to be released. I'll let you know. Got your number, haven't I? Right!"

With that she made it very plain that she was a busy woman and it was time for us to go. But we didn't mind. It was the animals that were important, not us.

On the way back I said casually to Mum, "You know that woman that runs the place? Angel? She's Mr Hennessy's wife."

I was being a bit cunning. I wanted to see if Mum would react. Like, maybe, her face might betray her true feelings, that is, DISAPPOINTMENT at Mr Hennessy being married. That would be a Good Sign as it would mean she was starting to go off Beastly

Bernard and take an interest in Mr Hennessy instead.

Unfortunately, Jilly went and ruined it. Before Mum could register any sort of emotion at all she interferingly chirped, "They're getting divorced, though."

Mum said, "I'm not surprised."

"Why aren't you?" I said.

"Well, frankly, I don't see how anyone could possibly live with the woman."

I frowned. On the one hand I thought that this could undoubtedly be taken as a Good Sign (Mum being on Mr Hennessy's side) but on the other hand I desperately didn't want to be disloyal to Angel.

"She just happens to feel very strongly about animals," I said. "She is absolutely brilliant with animals."

"Clara, there is more to life than just being brilliant with animals," said Mum.

I suppose she is right.

Maybe!

Chapter 8

Sometimes you feel as if your heart could just burst with the sheer *happiness* of everything.

I got home from school one day and Mum said that "that woman from the wild life place" had rung.

"Oh!" I said. "Is it Foxglove?"

"They're going to release her. Next weekend. Sunday morning. I suppose," said Mum, "you'll want to be there."

"And Jilly!" I said.

"Yes. Well. The only thing is, they're planning to do it in the early hours. About four o'clock, if you please."

I nodded. I could see that that would be better for Foxglove rather than waiting till daytime. No people about!

"Clara, I really do not want," said Mum, "to have to get up at four o'clock on a Sunday morning."

"That's all right," I said. "We'll walk."

"You will not walk. It will still be dark."

"But, Mum, we've got to be there! Mum, we've got to!"

"And what do we do with Benjy?"

"He could come with us! He'd love it! It would be dead exciting for him. It would be an *experience*. Oh, Mum, please!"

"What do I get in return?" said Mum.

"Undying love and gratitude!"

"Is that all?"

What more did she want?

"I think I'd rather you promised to tidy your bedroom and help wash up the breakfast things," said Mum.

Well! It seemed a bit squalid to me – I mean, in comparison with love and gratitude – but I had to promise. I think I'd have promised anything to be able to go and see Foxglove being released!

Jilly was as excited as I was. The following

day, which was Saturday, we bumped into Mr Hennessy in the village and told him about it.

"It's next Sunday," I said. "Are you going to come?"

Mr Hennessy pulled a face. "Do I have to?"

"No, of course not!" said Jilly; and she trod rather heavily on my big toe.

"I thought you might find it interesting," I said.

"*Clara*," said Jilly; and she trod on me again, even more heavily this time. "When people are getting divorced they don't like having to see each other."

"Oh! Sorry," I said. "I'd forgotten."

"Don't apologize," said Mr Hennessy. "It's getting up at four o'clock in the morning that bothers me. I know I am a totally idle sloth, but ... listen! I've been thinking. About that three-legged dog you wanted me to have—"

"Not three-*legged*," I said.

"No?"

"No!"

"One-eyed?"

"*No!*"

"Deaf?"

141

Solemnly, we shook our heads.

"Blind? Ancient? Funny?" said Mr Hennessy. "I could have sworn you said there was something wrong with it."

"It's a pit bull terrier," I said.

"And she's gorgeous," said Jilly.

"But just so terribly sad."

"Because she's been there for *months*."

"Because people are scared of her."

"Which is ridiculous," said Jilly, "because there is absolutely *nothing* to be scared of."

"Why? Has she had all her teeth removed?"

"No!" I was indignant. What a thing to suggest! And then I realized that Mr Hennessy had just been pulling my leg.

"Take me there," he said. "I'll have her."

We couldn't believe it!

"You mean, like ... right this minute?" said Jilly.

"Right this minute! Before I change my mind and buy myself a toy poodle."

"You couldn't have a toy poodle." Jilly said it earnestly. "You need a man's dog."

"So, all right! Let's go and get me one!"

We all rushed back across the Green to
Honeypot Lane so that I could tell Mum where
we were going and Mr Hennessy could get his
car. Then off we whizzed to End of the Line,
where we introduced Mr Hennessy to Meg.

Mr Hennessy said, "I've been told you have a
three-legged, one-eyed, blind, deaf, and
exceedingly ancient pit bull terrier without any
teeth that I have to give a home to."

Meg blinked.

"He's only joking," I said, hastily.

"You'd better come and see her," said Meg.
"See how you get on."

"You'll adore her," I whispered. "Honestly!"

And oh, I was right! It was love at first sight.
Dixie took one look at Mr Hennessy and just
went wild with sheer doggy delight, hurling
herself across her pen and scrabbling frantically
at the wire mesh in her eagerness to say hallo.
Her tail was going in circles, wagging her bum
along with it.

Meg brought her out on the lead and told Mr
Hennessy to take her into the field and get to
know her a bit.

"See if you're right for each other."

There was never any doubt. That funny dog, with her big clumpy head and cavernous mouth full of teeth, acted like Mr Hennessy was Prince Charming coming to claim her. He was her hero, the one she had been waiting for. She fawned and she flattered and she rolled on her back, and all the time she was making these little whimpering sounds of joy. She was a real man's dog!

"Looks like she's adopted me," said Mr Hennessy.

Meg smiled. "They do!"

And then she went on to say how Dixie had been registered with the police, which every pit bull or pit bull type has to be by law, and how she had to be muzzled all the time she was outside otherwise she could be "taken into custody" and even destroyed. For a moment I was worried that it might put Mr Hennessy off, which I do believe would have broken poor Dixie's heart.

But in spite of his jokiness he had obviously fallen for her in as big a way as she had fallen for him. It was just that being a man he couldn't admit it. Men are really odd like that. Even our lovely Mr Hennessy.

On the way home Jilly said, "We'd better not tell my mum she's a pit bull. She'd only freak."

"Yes," I said, "like Beastly Bernard. He says they're devil dogs."

Poor Dixie! She was cuddled up against me and it would have been hard to find anything less like a devil dog. I now know what it means when people say, *give a dog a bad name*. It is so unfair!

Of course Mr Hennessy wanted to know who Beastly Bernard was and so I had to explain.

"Only I think Mum might be going off him," I said, crossing my fingers for luck. Mum *couldn't* marry someone like the Beast! Our lives would be a total misery.

After that we tried to decide what we were going to tell Jilly's mum about Dixie.

"Do we have to tell her anything?" said Mr Hennessy.

Jilly said yes, because Dixie was a kind of odd-looking dog and her mum might say just out of interest "What breed is it?" and if Jilly said she was a pit bull terrier then her mum would go, like, help, screech, danger, save me!

Mr Hennessy agreed we couldn't have that, and so we decided that officially Dixie would be "a bitsa hound".

"Bits o' this, bits o' that," said Mr Hennessy. Which was in fact quite true, since a pit bull is not an actual genuine breed in the way, for instance, that a German Shepherd is.

And so the bitsa hound was rescued from her lonely pen and came to live with Mr Hennessy, and Jilly and me congratulated ourselves that that was yet another animal we had saved. We were getting really experienced! Now all we had to do was see Foxglove safely released back into the wild. Everything was working out so well!

And then we had this bitter blow.

It was Monday afternoon, the first day of the summer holidays, and Jilly was round at my place. We were in my bedroom, cutting out animal pictures to make a collage, when Mum called up the stairs, "Girls! There's someone to see you."

It was Darren. We were really surprised, especially as he was looking quite agitated.

"Got summat to tell yer," he said.

We all went into the garden, and it was there that Darren blurted out the terrible news: they were shooting foxes up on the golf course.

"Who is?" I said, shocked.

"Golf club. They were up there last night."

"The *golf* club? Shooting *foxes*?"

"Yeah. Well, they got these men. Men with guns. My uncle—" Darren stopped. His face had turned bright scarlet. He mumbled, "My uncle was up there. I went with 'im. I seen what they was doin'. They was shootin' the foxes an' then they got these terriers an' they was diggin' out the cubs an'—"

Jilly screamed and clapped her hands to her ears.

"No! Don't tell me! I don't want to know!"

Darren looked at me. His bottom lip was trembling.

"They use 'em," he whispered. "Use 'em to practise on."

I swallowed. Jilly still had her hands clamped over her ears.

"It ain't right," said Darren. "It didn't oughta be allowed!"

"But—" I took a breath, trying to stop my voice from wobbling. "Are you sure it's the golf club?"

"Yeah." Darren nodded. "They're goin' up there again tonight."

I turned and ran indoors.

"Mum!" I bawled. "They're shooting all the foxes over the golf course! Can I ring Bernard and get him to stop it?"

Mum was in the middle of one of her translations. She hates to be disturbed when she's wrestling with a translation.

"Bernard's a busy man," she said. "I'd rather you didn't bother him."

"But, Mum, they're shooting them! They'll shoot Foxglove's husband! And all her babies!"

"We don't know that she had any babies. Oh, look, Clara, I'm sorry, but I really don't know what you think Bernard can do about it."

"He's a member of the golf club!"

"Well, leave it till this evening and I'll have a word with him."

148

"This evening will be too late! They've got to be stopped *now*."

Mum sighed. "In that case, why don't you try the RSPCA and see what they can do?"

RSPCA! You can never get through to the RSPCA. And anyway, we had to take action straight away.

I rushed back out to the garden.

"Let's go to your place," I said to Jilly. "I'm going to ring Bernard!"

I knew I couldn't do it in front of Mum, but I was determined to do it.

Well! I got through to his office and the snooty person who answered the telephone put me through to an even snootier person who wanted to know who I was. So I said, "Could you please say that it's Clara, Mrs Carter's daughter, and that it's really really urgent." So then Beastly Bernard comes on the line and irritably says, "Clara? What's the matter?" and I babble at him about the foxes and he goes, "It's nothing whatsoever to do with me. I'm not on the Committee; I didn't make the decision. Take it up with the Committee," and bangs the phone down.

"What did he say?" said Jilly.

"He's not going to do anything. It's up to us!"

"Us?" said Darren. "What can we do?"

"I know what we can do! We can – we can ring the local paper and say we're having a demo!"

They gaped at me.

"What sort of demo?"

"Against the golf club! We'll make a banner and we'll march up there, amongst all the golfers, and stop them playing. The paper can come and take pictures and then they'll be too *ashamed* to go on killing!"

And that is exactly what we did. First of all I rang the *Gazette* and said what was happening and that we were going to be marching up to the golf course in one hour's time.

The reporter said, "Are you a local group?" I said, "Yes! We're Animal Lovers."

"And how many of you will be there, do you think?"

"Oh! Dozens," I said. I said that because I thought he might not come if he knew there were only three of us. "We're demonstrating against animal cruelty and we'd like you to come and take a picture for your newspaper."

"Could I ask how old you are?" said the reporter.

I thought quickly. "Um ... sixteen and a half," I said.

He seemed to find this amusing, for some reason. He said, "Sixteen and a half, eh? OK! I'll see if we can get someone up there."

Meanwhile, Jilly and Darren had found some sheets of cardboard, nailed them to some wooden sticks that were in the garden shed and were busily painting slogans in bright red paint (which Jilly's mum had used for her front door).

These were the slogans that they painted:

The one about killing babies was Jilly's idea and she was so proud of it that I didn't like to point out she'd spelt the word infanticide wrongly. It would have seemed rather mean. And anyway, it wasn't really important. What was important was saving the foxes.

I tore back next door and yelled at Mum that I was going on a demo and she said, "Are you? That's nice. Enjoy yourself," thus betraying the fact that she hadn't heard a word I'd said. Which was probably just as well or she might have tried to stop me.

We tore like the wind up to the golf course. You're not supposed to walk over there while they're playing golf, but we didn't care! Boldly we marched across the grass, right in front of a woman who was waggling her bottom over a golf ball, the way that they do before they hit them. She saw us and yelled, "What are you kids doing here? You'll get yourselves hurt!"

Another woman, who was with her, waved her golf club at us and shouted, "Move, move, before you get hit!"

It was a bit scary, but we stood our ground.

"You're killing babies!" bellowed Jilly.

"You're no better than murderers!" I bawled.

Darren didn't bellow or bawl anything, but he stood beside us and bravely held up his banner.

By now, some other women had come out of the club house, attracted by the noise. And oh, bliss! A man with a camera had appeared!

"Are you the *Gazette*?" I demanded.

"Yes," he said. "Are you the demo?"

"Yes!"

We waved our placards at him.

"Sixteen and a half going on eleven," he muttered; but he pointed his camera at us and took some pictures!

"What's happening? What's going on?"

All the women golfers had come crowding round us. We had thought they would be angry, but most of them seemed more curious than anything.

We told them about the foxes being shot and the poor little baby fox cubs being dug out and thrown to the terriers, and they started fiercely muttering amongst themselves and accusing "the Committee" of acting high-handedly and going behind their backs.

The woman who had waved her golf club at us snapped, "Don't you worry! We'll soon get this sorted out," and went striding back into the club house.

The reporter asked the other women if what we had said was true, and one of them admitted that it might be.

"There was some talk of it."

"But why?" screamed Jilly. "What do you want to kill them for?"

"Well, because they – they ruin the greens. They dig. They—"

"They steal golf balls!"

"Yes, they do. They steal golf balls."

"And they leave mess."

"You kill them just for that?" I couldn't believe it! Golf after all is only a *game*. Foxes are living creatures.

There were just these two women who seemed to be against us. All the rest were on our side! Some of them, I could tell, were just as horrified as we were at what was being done.

The woman who had gone marching into the club house came marching out again. She said,

"Right! That's seen to that. You can call off your demo. There will be no more shooting of foxes by this golf club. That is *official*."

I don't know who the woman was but she must have been quite important because no one tried arguing with her. The two that were against us did a bit of muttering, but only half-heartedly. I think even they were secretly rather ashamed. I mean, shooting fox cubs just because they stole a few golf balls!

I knew what Angel would have said...

When we got home Mum told me that Bernard had rung her and asked her to inform me that the golf club were perfectly within their rights to protect their property and there was nothing that I or anyone else could do to stop them. To which I merely said, "Hah! That's all he knows."

"Clara," said Mum, sharply. "What have you been up to?"

"Stopping people *murdering*!" I said.

When the local paper came out on Friday, there were me, Jilly and Darren with our placards staring out from the front page. Was Mum surprised! And was Bernard *furious*! He came round that evening and I heard him complaining to Mum about my behaviour, and then I heard Mum say something about it being my "democratic right" to stage a peaceful protest. I was really glad that she was sticking up for me. It gave me hope that my daydream about her and Mr Hennessy might come true one day after all.

Next morning when Jilly and I took Mud for his walk, we bumped into Mr Hennessy with the bitsa hound, and she and Mud played together ever so happily. Mr Hennessy had seen our photo in the paper. He congratulated us and said, "I'll bring along my copy to give to Angel, shall I?"

"You mean you're coming, after all?" cried Jilly.

"How could I not?" said Mr Hennessy. "You've shamed me into it!"

So Sunday morning, just before dawn, Mum and me and Jilly, and Benje and Mr Hennessy and Angel, all gathered up by the golf course to say farewell to Foxglove as we sent her home. Angel brought her out of the van in her travelling cage and Mr Hennessy carried it to the edge of the woods. Angel opened the lid –

and that was that! Foxglove streaked for cover, and was gone.

"Well! Was it really worth all that effort?" said Mum, later.

I told her that it was. I said that you couldn't expect gratitude from a wild creature. It was enough that you had helped it survive and get back to where it belonged.

It was only to Jilly that I admitted I would love to be able to see Foxglove again, just one more time, to know that she was all right.

I didn't think I ever would. But then one night, about a fortnight later, I was woken by strange sounds coming from the garden. I tiptoed across to the window to look, and there in the moonlight I saw these two little fox cubs playing on the grass. They had one of Mud's toys and they were pulling at it, shaking it, making mock growly sounds as they danced around on their long trembly legs.

I knew that I had to wake Jilly! We didn't have our fox pull any more, but I couldn't bear for her not to see, so I rushed to the corner of the room and thumped just as hard as ever I could on the wall. Then I went racing back again to the window, just in time to see a dark shape emerge from the bushes. Another fox! My thumping must have alerted her. She had obviously come to collect the cubs, to tell them that it was time to go, because they obediently dropped the toy and went lolloping off towards the wall. One after the other they scuttled back over it. The mother fox followed. And, oh! She had a white tip to her tail...

"It was Foxglove, wasn't it?" said Jilly next morning. "She came back to us!"

Foxglove and her babies. And we had both seen her!

"It was what I wanted more than *anything*," said Jilly.

Me, too! After all that we had been through, it was a truly happy ending. For us *and* for Foxglove.